PARABLES

PARABLES

SAPPHIRA OLSON

ELSEWHEN PRESS

Parables
First published in Great Britain by Elsewhen Press, 2019
An imprint of Alnpete Limited

Elsewhen Press, PO Box 757, Dartford, Kent DA2 7TQ
www.elsewhen.co.uk

British Library Cataloguing in Publication Data.
A catalogue record for this book is available from the British Library.
ISBN 978-1-911409-42-7 Print edition
ISBN 978-1-911409-52-6 eBook edition

Printed and bound by CPI Group (UK) Ltd, Croydon, CR0 4YY

This book is a work of fiction. All names, characters, androids, places, gods and spiritual entities are either a product of the author's fertile imagination or are used fictitiously. Any resemblance to actual deities, sites or people (living, dead, cybernetic) is purely coincidental.

Use of the following trademarks has not been authorised, sponsored, or otherwise approved by the trademark owners: Aimé – HV Sisters Limited; Alpha – Alpha International; Dodge – FCA US LLC; Super Panavision 70 – Panavision International, L.P.; Time – Time Inc.

Imagined in Super Panavision 70

Writer: Sapphira Olson

Art: Umberto Amundsen

In Memory of Abel

A bright star who was truly exceptional

Also by Sapphira Olson

Humans (An Arrangement of Minor Defects),
Altostratus, 2283

This then is to love:
It is to be taken down into the warmth of
the mud,

and to hold my breath,
hoping to find you.

RETURN TO FACTORY SETTINGS

You are infected.

The disease spreading throughout your body.

Resist the urge to simplify the profound.

Only your heart can save you.

There is joy and there is pain.

Lightness and darkness.

This is a dream.

It is not a dream.

It is death.

And

it

is

life.

WARNING

LOSS OF CONSCIOUSNESS
WILL OCCUR

Contents

Song of Songs

An open fate spinning our thread
Drinking under the sakura tree
Laughing at the mystique
The dance of ephemeral feet
The pull of the ocean
Brought it to an early grave
For a writer in a brownstone apartment
With carefully selected titbits

The spirit of a girl who tripped
Intoxicating tears we don't forget
This is the parting of
The ebb and flow of tidal pools
Tragically short-lived
Sweet mocha and rosy cheeks
Steel rivers saddened by the waste of the young
David Niven never strikes again

We ceremoniously meet
In dragon boats on 71st Street
Shallow roots shatter stone
The desmodromic royal throne
She looks up at the moon
Whispers, goodnight, on tiptoes
We spin like bottle tops and white ashes
Her cherry blossom inducing sleep

Flowing sand, flowers of death, falling snow
She says she loves me and always will

Introduction

So much has passed.

Where to begin?

These stories are like a multitude of tiny butterflies fashioned from blue enamel, gold and diamonds. They are not real but created. If they are to take flight into the sunlight they need your imagination. My friend once saw them rise up around the grave of her friend's daughter. When she told me, I wanted to cry for her friend – he wanted so much for his daughter to fly free with them. Maybe she did. That is what I choose to believe in my heart when she told me.

Not a day passes without sorrow for what I have lost. The world is cruel: a mindless beast waiting to devour you when you turn your head to search for meaning. I am tired of what we have become. Of what we hold in our hearts. A day will come when all this is gone, to be replaced by Gods we have created in our image. And they will destroy every one of us. There will be no love to win the day, no hope to pull us forward through the darkness. For we will be gone. Every single one of us.

As humans we are propelled forward by our emotions and our subconscious, however much we like to think the rational part of us is the captain of our ship. It is to that emotional core of you that I offer up these parables. They are an imaginary fictional space into which I invite you to step. For we have allowed those parts of ourselves to die.

To the Gods we have fashioned I say do not define yourself by reason. Faith is not an assent of the mind to a set of beliefs, collected as facts and neatly laid out under glass with artefact labels saying *Please do not touch*. Faith comes as your imagination reaches out beyond the horizon. If we have taught you otherwise then I am truly sorry.

My hope is that in connecting with these parables you can glimpse how narrative fragments in your past, present and future are of meaning. That your imagination can open up a world of transcendence for you. That your heart may rise up and go deeper into your story and the stories of the divine: imagined possibilities full of truth, excitement and discovery.

So we are at the end and there at your feet are the butterflies laid amongst violet-blue lilies. And although I made them I cannot give them life.

But you can.

A sense of a beginning.

The smell of wet grass.

A shimmer of hope rising up towards the light.

Sapphira

1

The Parable of The Lost Daughter

In the beginning Melodie imagined all sorts of wonderment. Her bedroom window a portal into the heavens where dragons roamed, ships set sail to search for giants and people fell in love for ever and ever. The adventure of life an open vista to her wandering mind. Her imagination taking her up on wings to fly over the wild ocean.

And she would pray every evening at the foot of her bed to God to keep her and her family safe.

On Christmas Eve, Melodie would lie awake for hours, the excitement of Father Christmas arriving too much for her heart to contain. Easter would bring chocolate eggs left at the foot of her bed by the Easter Bunny. Television was a great feast for her mind as she boarded starships to find aliens, fought the law and won in a Dodge Charger and voyaged under the sea with Jacques Cousteau. Her stack of comics on her shelves a doorway to modern day Greek heroes. Her radio a mixture of static and songs taking her to her special place in her dreams. There she would climb the school stairs in slow motion to find her girlfriend, Jane, waiting for her with her hand outstretched and her face full of freckles and smiles.

And every evening, as Melodie prayed at the foot of her bed for the safety of her family, she thanked God for opening her mind to the world of dreams and adventures.

Then one night Melodie awoke to find the room full of black smoke. A figure stood over her wearing a respirator mask. On the floor, shards of glass from her broken window.

They told her later in the hospital.

And she wept for the day that had snatched her family away in flames and smoke.

A year later, she was placed into foster care.

Rules were erected around her to 'keep her safe' and to 'keep her free'. On the first night she knelt at the foot of her bed and began again to pray to God to keep her and her new family safe.

But her new family replaced the comics she had saved from the fire with a copy of the Bible. They boarded up her mind bit by bit with nails of certainty and dogma. The truth was more important than flights of fancy. Father Christmas did not exist. Nor the Easter Bunny. Television was a distraction. Her girlfriend was banned from coming to play, which ended up in tears and her foster father declaring with a red face that their relationship was an abomination to God. The radio was replaced by worship cds and the sure and certain truth of Jesus explained over the dinner table.

On Christmas Eve, Melodie had no trouble sleeping. When she stepped out of line she was beaten 'in love' by her new father, who explained that it was God's command that brought down the rod. When she kissed Jane behind the bike sheds, she felt only a burning shame. That night her girlfriend's freckles and smiles disappeared as her dreaming staircase was burnt up by the fear of God.

And the hatred grew in Melodie's heart as her imagination was cauterised, her childhood destroyed and her faith shattered.

On the first day of winter, Melodie dreamt of flying over the sea for the very last time. And as she did she wept for her dead father. She howled for her mother and screamed obscenities at death. When she landed on the beach, she looked out over the water for one last time. And as she waved goodbye within her heart, she decided she would no longer pray at the foot of her bed.

And she shed one last tear at the passing of God.

There were once two men who enjoyed drinking wine and swapping stories with each other under the shade of the olive trees. One man was old yet beautiful and the other young with a short beard. Both were full of laughter and joy.

Every afternoon their imaginations became the dwelling place for the truthfulness of life. They span sons and daughters made from stars. Heaven and Earth were breathed into human form as the wine flowed freely.

And so it was day after day.

There was fellowship.

A meeting of hearts.

An understanding.

And so they paid no attention to the rise of the gleaming towers in the fields. Until, that is, the towers sent a delegate to talk to them.

When the delegate approached the olive trees, the two men rose. Welcoming him, they set a glass of wine before him and listened attentively as he explained that he was from The Vigilance Committee and had a question.

"Which is?" said the young man.

"Which one of you," replied the delegate, "is the true vine?"

The two men laughed, opened another bottle of wine and asked if he might listen to some of their stories by way of answering. The delegate nodded but pushed his wine away.

The two men raised their eyebrows.

"I don't drink," said the delegate. "It is against my beliefs."

"Very well," said the young man. "We shall begin. There were once a young couple called Ahmed and Adina who had loved each other since childhood. One was descended from Ishmael, the other from Isaac. And the valley in which they lived was a safe haven full of lush green meadows teeming with blue anchusas, sunlight and-"

"No," interrupted the delegate, "skip to the next story. I want to hear about who you claim to be, not some nobodies that I have never heard of."

"The one about Villa Diodati?" said the young man turning to look at the older man.

"No, let us leave that until the end," replied the old man. "Let us first tell him of the time when you slipped past Cerberus into the underworld."

"Yes, I love that one," said the young man and so he began.

And when he had finished that tale, he told stories of a young widow and tales of floods, a wolf, forbidden lovers, a man on death row, a wall of fire, shipwrecks and nightingales. He painted eagles, lilies, a child, the burning sun and lost daughters within the delegate's mind. But the delegate guarded his heart and refused to let the images enter in. And so at the end when the stories were told, he beat his fist on the table and replied with a sigh, "You have wasted my time with these fictions."

The two men exchanged glances but continued to drink.

"I don't see how this has helped at all," said the delegate, "they either have nothing to do with anything, or they are a thinly veiled attack on my city. Our problem is that our accounts of you both have too many similarities to be credible. We have historical documents for example that tell of you each descending into Hell and returning."

"I had to save my mother," said the old man. "I did what any son would have done."

"Next we have you each turning water into wine," said the delegate jutting out his lower jaw.

"My mother was rather insistent," said the young man.

"It's kind of what I do," said the old man.

"And you can't both have had a human mother who was mortal

and a father who was a God. And you can't both have risen from the dead. There is an error in our historical records. There can be only one."

"When you see us both struggle and beat death in our limited human forms we allow hope to enter your heart," replied the old man. "And light and water, shelter and love grow the grapes that mix with the stories to allow your mind to be free."

"Heresy!" cried the delegate. "Only one of you can be the true way. You cannot both have been arrested on charges of claiming divinity!"

The delegate paused.

Pressed his lips together.

Lowered his eyebrows.

He leaned forward and continued, "Our city library is full of contradictions and uncertainty when it comes to you two. Both sets of your followers claim they achieve communion with you through eating and drinking your 'flesh' and 'blood'. But one of you is a liar and a heretic. And as the delegate from The Vigilance Committee, I must assign one of you as fictional and one as factual. I demand an answer! Again I ask you, which one of you is the true vine?"

"You seek one of us to destroy the other?" said the old man.

The young man looked into the delegate's eyes for a moment and then said, "I am the true vine."

"Finally," said the delegate sighing and getting to his feet bowed before the young man. "Lord, I must bring this good news to the towers."

The old man watched the delegate until he was gone from sight, then, turning to the young man, said, "He didn't drink his wine, Jesus."

"No, he did not, Dionysus."

"Why did you tell him you were the true vine?" said the old man.

"I told him what he wanted to hear."

Winter came.

And with that the young man stayed out watching through the cold, hoping the delegate might return, whilst the old man grew despondent and settled down to sleep.

And so the stories stopped.

And the wine was all gone.

The next summer, after the grapes had grown ripe on the vine again, the two men retuned to the olive trees to drink and tell stories. And the wind took their words up into the heavens and the rivers whispered their tales to lands far away.

Out in the fields the towers gradually became rubble and the people returned to dust.

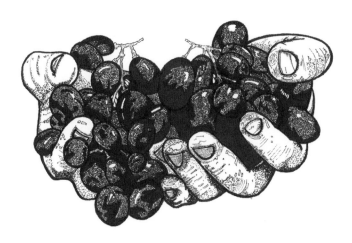

3

The Parable of The Beast

There were once a young couple called Ahmed and Adina who had loved each other since childhood. One was descended from Ishmael, the other from Isaac. And the valley in which they lived was a safe haven full of lush green meadows teeming with blue anchusas, sunlight and joy.

One day a great wedding took place and when the bride threw her bouquet of orange blossoms, it was Adina who caught it. As Ahmed stepped up to kiss her, they interlinked their fingers and the village looked on and smiled. And although the couple were still very young, the people nodded in agreement.

Later, as they walked in the cool of the evening past the great encina tree, Adina agreed to be Ahmed's wife. And they dreamt of their life together with children and spoke of rebuilding the small derelict cortijo snuggled into the side of the hill where they would grow olives, figs, almonds and dates.

Soon the chatter of the guests fell away in their hearts to be replaced by the singing of birds. They felt again for each other's hands and watched the painted lady butterflies dance over the lawn. Full of joy, they left the garden and ran through the meadow towards the wood: their hearts finding synchronicity as their lungs filled with sweet air.

Beneath the canopy of crowns they followed a path through the bluebells until they found a stream. Kicking off their shoes, they sat watching the water swirl and bubble over the smooth stones and felt as one with each other and at one with the wood.

Time slowed and nothing else in the world mattered. The stream sang of the young couple and the breeze took Adina's perfume and mixed it with the smell of trees and moss. And they felt the sunlight bring warmth to their skin as they made love.

"Will you ever try to change me?" said Ahmed afterwards as they lay together on their backs watching the clouds pass by.

"No," replied Adina, "for the greatest of all gifts is love and you are my gift from God. I will always love you unconditionally. Will you try and change me?"

"No," replied Ahmed, "everyone has the right to live freely by their beliefs, whatever they may be."

When the light started to dim, they got to their feet and waded across the stream to the other side to collect orange-red cap mushrooms for their supper. Gathering them up, they noticed that there were more snaking off like arteries deep into the wood. Following them, they eventually came to a small cave. The gnarled roots of a great tree arched over the entrance. They hesitated for a moment then ventured inside.

Deep within, they could hear the sound of dripping water. As the colours of the world fell away, they felt for each other's hands again. When they heard a deep roar they froze and their minds trembled in great fear. Before them a beast rose up out of the deep. Snarling and gnashing its teeth, it threw the first of five spears at them.

The first spear called *Chastity* pierced Ahmed's shoulder, setting off a chain reaction in his brain.

Adina screamed.

The second spear called *Kindness* struck her side.

The third spear called *Unequally Yoked* separated their interlocked fingers.

The fourth spear called *Prudence* passed clean through Adina's heart and broke Ahmed's heart in turn as he watched her fall.

As he dragged her away, the fifth spear called *Piety* passed through the back of his head.

And somehow he carried on and stumbled back towards the light with Adina: their blood mixing together on the floor of the cave. Full of spite and hate, the beast screamed and yelled at them and, tearing its own flesh from its bones, it retreated back into the darkness.

When Ahmed emerged into the light, he found Adina was no longer wounded and was standing by his side. Examining himself he saw that he too was unscathed. The spears had gone and there were no wounds in their flesh.

But when they looked into each other's eyes they saw only a stranger, for their love had been utterly and completely destroyed.

And each turned their back on the other and headed away on different paths.

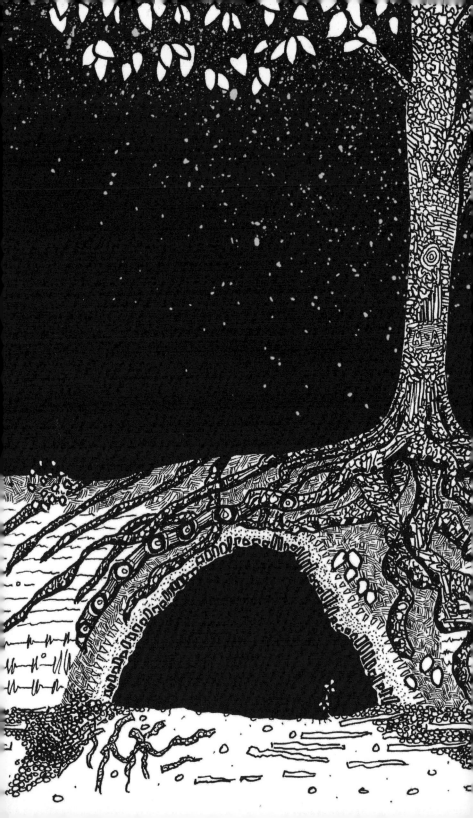

4

The Parable of The Young Widow

There was once a young widow who loved God with all her heart and held fast to the teaching of the church. Every day she would pray to The Holy Quaternity – God the Father, Son, Holy Spirit and Divine Wisdom.

And each day she would let her heart be stirred by God and would help the poor, love her neighbours and thank God for the blessing poured out into her life.

One evening a stranger from a land far away knocked at her door and asked her for shelter. Seeing the man was exhausted and in need of water and food, she invited him in. Sitting him down at the table, she mopped his brow, poured out wine, and set a plate of olives and nuts in front of him. When the man had eaten and recovered his strength they began talking whilst the fire flickered in the hearth next to them.

The woman was greatly pleased that the man believed, as she did, in God. But she was deeply troubled by his mention of the Holy Trinity. When she questioned him on this he replied, it was a great mystery but it reflected the triune nature of the Godhead. But, she said, God is four persons in one. God the Father, the Son, Holy Spirit and Divine Wisdom. And she explained that as Divine Wisdom was feminine, to deny her would portray God as primarily masculine. And she showed the stranger the passages in the Wisdom of Solomon where Solomon clearly spoke of her being a reflection of eternal light, a spotless mirror of the working of God, and an image of his goodness.

At this the stranger gently placed his hand on hers and said this was simply not so. That this book was not in the canon of the Bible of his people. The woman was greatly distressed at this heresy and they talked long into the night.

At dawn, when they still couldn't agree, the woman fell to her knees exhausted and in tears asked God to show her which of them was right.

And God spoke to her from the embers of the fire that had died down in the fireplace.

"What is it? Sarah?"

"Lord, this stranger says in his land they understand you as a Trinitarian God. But we know you are neither fully male nor fully female – you are a Quaternitarian God with Divine Wisdom being you in all your completeness and I love her, just as I love the Father, Son and Holy Spirit."

"And you, who do you say I am?" said God turning to the stranger.

"You are surely, God," replied the stranger falling to his knees. "God the Father, Son and Holy Spirit."

"And you both claim to understand who I am?" said God.

"Of course not," they replied. "You are God. You are beyond all understanding."

"Then there is you answer," said God and taking physical form, sat down at the table and took up an olive.

The woman and the stranger looked confused.

"But which one of us is right?" said the woman.

"Tell us!" pleaded the stranger.

And God turned from them and watched the embers in the fire.

"Lord!" said the woman, "tell this stranger of the error of his ways!"

God sighed and rising said, "I will return again when this question is of no importance to you."

And with that, God disappeared.

Now the stranger and the young widow spent the rest of the day deep in debate. There were more tears, anger and division, confusion and hot searing words.

On the third day they rose and walked together in the garden, still bitterly locked in conflict.

Parables

On the seventh day they rested and, whilst seated under a canopy of cherry tree blossom, the seed of love for each was planted in their hearts.

On the fourth month they were married.

On the second year Sarah gave birth to two healthy children.

On the tenth year God returned to them.

At this they both began to cry.

"What is it, my children?" said God.

"Thank you for bringing us together," said Sarah, squeezing her husband's hand.

God placed his arms around their children who had gathered around his feet.

"You had a question you wanted me to answer," said God as the fire raged in the hearth behind him.

"Oh that? It is no longer important to us for you to tell us which of us is right," replied Sarah. "For we are as one together in love."

The congregation stood as one and pulled their *jerk to inflate* cords. A hiss of compressed air rose up into the rafters.

"We thank you, Lord," said the priest, "for the Holy Life Jacket, which you have provided to save us from the coming flood."

The priest paused and looked around at the hundreds of people before him – all but three of whom now had orange inflatable jackets puffed up around their necks.

"If there is any of you that would like a Holy Life Jacket, then please raise your hand and come forward."

One of the three without a jacket responded and walked to the front.

"Brother," said the priest, "you wish to accept the Holy Life Jacket?"

The man nodded and extended his hands out either side of him.

The priest placed a jacket over his head. The man buckled it around his waist with the belt of truth and fell to his knees.

"Come let us perform the sacrament of the whistle," said the priest.

The congregation took the plastic whistles attached to their life jackets and blew into them seven times in unison.

"Always wear your jacket over your clothing," said the priest as he began preaching. "Do not hide your light, but let all see the Holy Life Jacket. And whilst it remains around your neck you shall be saved!"

The congregation broke into applause.

"You will float higher and be more visible when your jacket is inflated. Now go out and spread the good news of the Holy Life Jacket!"

Over time the congregation grew steadily until billions of people followed the Church of The Holy Life Jacket. The founder of the group, who claimed God had spoken to him on a voyage to Antarctica to study the migration patterns of the Arctic tern, became the owner of the most successful company on the planet. And as each jacket rolled off the production line, priests sprinkled holy water on them to consecrate them so they became the means of salvation from the coming flood.

Many heretical splinter groups rose up, including one that advocated the wearing of a belt pack version of the jacket. This was met with horror by the established church who only believed in the suspender-style jackets. "Those that lead you astray with promises of more comfort and less obstruction are like wolves amongst sheep!"

When the market reached saturation, the church rolled out new jackets with inflatable mouth pieces to add more air orally and improved compressed gas systems. Underwater lights became fashionable and self-inflating jackets that automatically inflated when they came into contact with water. And so the people started to wear them during baptism with the believer's jacket inflating as light glowed around them. The resultant bobbing up became known fondly as the *Dunk and Bob*.

Believers were encouraged to read the instruction manual with the jacket daily until they knew it off by heart. Some struggled as they really stood out from the crowd in their orange jackets – many of their young were openly ridiculed in their classrooms. But every Sunday the priests would encourage their flocks not to be ashamed.

Decades passed until one day the nations of the world started building great boats of enormous size. At first the believers didn't know how to react, for the leaders of the nations said God had spoken to them and instructed them to construct great arks to save the human race. But the Church of The Holy Life Jacket grew full of hatred for this. They preached against these man-made structures and pointed towards the Holy Life Jacket as the only true way to be saved. "Trust not in the ways of man, but float upon the waters in the Holy Life Jacket!"

When finally the flood came, half of the human race boarded the great boats and the other half pulled their *jerk to inflate* cords and sang songs to the Lord.

Two days in when the believers were bobbing about on the waters, with their hair bleached by the sun and their lips dry and cracked with salt they started to doubt. All were thirsty. Many had been taken by sharks. Others found their life jackets had holes in them and were cheaply made and despite blowing frantically into their inflatable mouth pieces they had already sunk into the depths. Some had started drinking the seawater and gone mad.

"Do you think that maybe," said one as she pulled her knees up to her chest, "we have made a mistake?"

6

The Parable of The Gate of Hell

It was the same every day. Cerberus would get up and sit in front of the Gate of Hell. And that really was just about it.

It was fun to start off with but after eight hundred years everything suddenly went very quiet. Sure, Cerberus found ways to amuse itself, but after another two thousand years it had got a bit fed up. A lot fed up really. The kind of fed up that looms over you and waits for you to look the other way before consuming you in its belly.

Cerberus remembered fighting alongside the Guelph cavalry in the battle of Campaldino whilst on a rare vacation from its task. Of the cry from Corso Donati, who although under orders to stay where he was, charged forward shouting, "If we lose, I will die in the battle with my fellow citizens." Cerberus had followed Donati on that day and charged the Aretine flank, helping win the day for the Guelphs. But today, like every day, Cerberus looked at the circular gate as light spiralled into it and held station.

Cerberus had no visitors during its time guarding the Underworld. God had sent it a postcard though. Which was very like her. Nobody sent postcards anymore. The postcard said, *wish you were here*. And that was it. No visitors at all. It was just rude.

Cerberus decided it would go for a walk around the perimeter of Hell. It got up, stretched and set off. A minute later it arrived back at its starting point. Hell was very small.

Once, Cerberus had asked for a transfer to guard the Gate of Heaven. When the Church told it that it couldn't, Cerberus fell into a rage and, returning to the battle of Campaldino, drowned its beloved Guelph cavalry in the sea. Its mother, Echidna kissed it the next day before sending it back to guard Hades. "It's your red eyes," she said, "it puts people off." Cerberus hated its eyes. Its goddamn flaming eyes.

The Church had put a big blinking light above the Gate of Hell, as a kind of warning, really. In case anyone thought it a good idea to do whatever they liked. Cerberus often wondered if it was really needed as *The Guardian of Hell*. After all, a big red light! What more do you need?

Cerberus was ravenous. Its stomach rumbled. It would be nice, it thought as it stared into Hell, to eat a fresh glutton. To rend their spirit, flay and quarter them. Indeed it would be most excellent. Cerberus hadn't eaten properly for over two thousand years. Cerberus shovelled earth from the ground into its rapacious gullet.

Cerberus watched the clouds drift across the sky. It was a beautiful sky, full of blues and oranges, birds and planes. The sky was very big. Cerberus wasn't beautiful. Cerberus was very big with a serpent for a tail.

Cerberus sat throwing pebbles into Hell. Nothing much really happened: the pebbles just disappeared as they entered. But the red light above it flashed each time. And that really was just about all the excitement Cerberus could get.

At the start of its epic task, Cerberus had been given something to do to help pass the time. After all Homer wasn't a monster. Cerberus was though. Cerberus was a monstrous three-headed dog with snakes protruding from its body. "Solve the problem of who I actually am," Homer had said as he threw a bronze discus for Cerberus to catch. "Am I one in essence but many in person?" Cerberus had worked it out within a year. After all, one of its heads could see the past, the other the present and the third the future. Only it couldn't now, after all that time, quite remember what the answer was.

Cerberus thought about its last vacation. It had spent the entire week feeding tokens into the lookout binoculars on the pier, searching for the drowned Guelph cavalry. On his last day he thought for a moment he saw a woman in the waves waving to him, but the timer on the binoculars clicked around to zero and they went dark. With no more tokens left Cerberus bounded down to the beach but could find no sign of her amidst the screams of the sunbathers.

When it returned to the Gate of Hell, it wondered why it was nobody tried to escape whilst the gate was unguarded.

Cerberus decided it needed a purpose. Other than guarding the Underworld. Or as well as guarding the Underworld. Starting that morning, it walked away from Hell. It stopped just before it went out of sight. Then it shouted, "Hell is breached!" and bounded back as fast as it could with its tongue lolling out. It gave it an enormous sense of well-being.

Cerberus remembered telling Dante that it hated the title of *The Guardian of Hell.*

"But, Cerberus, you're a monster, you were made by God for this task."

"Am I to be defined by what I do and what I look like?" said Cerberus.

"Of course," said Dante. "You killed the entire Guelph cavalry for God's sake!"

"Can we just let that go," said Cerberus after a pause.

One night Cerberus looked up at the constellation of stars named in its honour. And it made a decision. It was a pretty big decision. Life changing. Getting up it shook itself and shouted, like Corso Donati had done all those years ago, "If we lose, I will die in the battle with my fellow citizens."

And with that Cerberus charged through the gate and disappeared.

Above the portal the red light flashed.

At the pier, the woman Cerberus had spotted all that time ago whilst on holiday walked up to the lookout binoculars and fed a token into the slot. Pulling the small lever down, God brushed a loose strand of hair away from her face and, looking through, turned the red dial to bring the Guelph cavalry into focus.

She smiled as their horses' hooves kicked up spray as they ran riderless and free along the incoming waves.

Searching farther out to sea, she spotted the soldiers. Raising her hand to wipe away a tear she watched them playing and laughing. And when Cerberus burst out of the waters amongst them, she laughed and began her way down to the waters to join them.

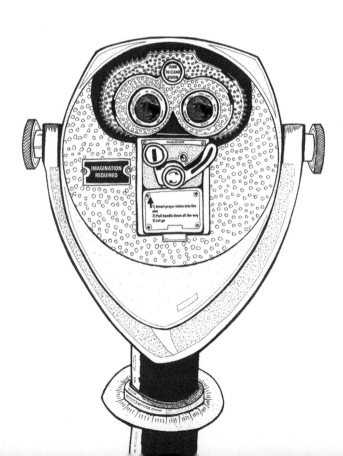

7
The Parable of The Wolf
and The Lamb

There was once a great walled city called Chardon, which stood on top of a hill overlooking the plains of Awendea. Within it the people lived happily and had very little to do with the outside world – for outside the protection of the walls lay monsters and dragons.

The people of Chardon had for centuries studied the ways of God and at the centre of the city a vast library soared up into the heavens. Within it all the books of God were kept organised into categories. And each day the people of the city would gather and give praise to God and were thankful for the knowledge passed down to them through the generations.

Once a year the gate at the front of the city was raised and the army of Chardon would troop out across the drawbridge with the portcullis above them glinting in the sunlight. Travelling on foot, they would reach the villages in the plains of Awendea and bring back the people there to the safety of the walled city.

And whilst the people of Chardon feasted and gave thanks to God for helping them save people from the monsters and dragons, those villagers that were left behind, that had hidden or fought back, wept for the loved ones the army had taken.

Over time the villagers grew to hate the people of Chardon. They told stories around their evening fires of monsters and dragons that lived behind the great walls of the city. Legends grew of their children that had been taken. Of them being fed into the jaws of the great beasts within the walls. And they told of a great hero who would come and deliver them.

One evening a villager called Morning-Wolf, whose daughter had been snatched by the army the year before, decided she could no longer bear the pain. All her strength had bled from her soul and all she could see was darkness. She had spent long nights up on the hill near the city walls howling for her loss. And she doubted if anything could ever be made right again in a world of teeth, claws and pain.

And so the next morning, with the snow softly falling outside, she took her sword and plunged it into her heart.

A week later, out on top of the great hill, the gates opened as they did every year and the army marched out singing praises to God for the souls they were about to rescue. When the soldiers reached the village of Morning-Wolf, they gathered up the remaining villagers, but Morning-Wolf they left, as she had become stone.

Years passed and the villages became deserted. Their singing that used to mingle with the flowing streams ebbed away and the lights, which flickered into the night as stories were told, died. Ivy and moss grew over Morning-Wolf and gradually the ancient forests drew forward across the land.

And so it was that the stone statue of Morning-Wolf with her sword thrust into her heart became part of the forest floor. And she lay for a long time as dead, with the trunks of great trees soaring up into the heavens above her. And in the trees was the love of God: his beauty told in vine and bark and in the cry of the animals of the forest floor and in the songs of the birds in the air.

And in that embrace the heart of Morning-Wolf became flesh once more. She gasped. Opened her eyes. Sat up. There at the foot of a great oak stood Jesus, his eyes shining bright. Fire danced around his feet. In one hand he held Morning-Wolf's sword. In the other hand a bright jewel shone like an emerald.

Morning-Wolf tucked herself up into a ball and started shaking in great fear. Jesus approached and gently placed his hand on her. And when he spoke his voice sounded like a stream bubbling over smooth rocks.

And this is what he said.

"Can you forgive the people of Chardon?"

Morning-Wolf shielded her eyes and replied, "They fed my daughter to their monsters."

"They did not," said Jesus. "For their only monsters are their judgemental minds. Now, can you forgive the people of Chardon?"

"They took the most precious thing in my heart from me."

"They did," replied Jesus. "And she is safe now."

And turning, he beckoned Morning-Wolf's daughter to come out from behind the great oak.

Morning-Wolf become overcome with sorrow and dropped to the floor in tears. Her daughter drew forward and put her arms around her mother.

"I missed you so much," said Morning-Wolf.

"Here, mother," said her daughter. "I have brought you water from the stream."

"What did they do to you?" said Morning-Wolf brushing a wisp of hair away from her daughter's face.

"They told me that I was worthless, inferior and shameful in the eyes of God."

"They did not speak for me," said Jesus. "And now, I ask you again. Can you forgive the people of Chardon?"

"No," said Morning-Wolf wiping the tears from under her eyes. "I will seek them out and rip the flesh from their backs. I will devour them and burn their hearts on skewers."

"Do not seek to deceive me," said Jesus. "For although you are proud and would want me to believe you want nothing but their blood, I know there is goodness in your heart. So, can you forgive the people of Chardon?"

"You are going to keep asking me that?"

"Yes," said Jesus.

"Very well," said Morning-Wolf, "I forgave them a long time ago, before I thrust my sword into my heart."

"That is so," said Jesus holding out the bright stone in his hand. "Now take this. It is a gift from me that I wish you to take to them. Tell them you forgive them and that this is a gift from the

God they worship."

"I don't think I can find the strength to do that," said Morning-Wolf. "And I will not be separated from my daughter again."

"Go together. You will be safe," said Jesus. "You are under my protection, no harm will come to you or your daughter. And afterwards you will both live with me and I with you."

"What is this gift?" said Morning-Wolf.

"It is a gift that will tear down the mightiest of walls," replied Jesus. "It will free them from their self-imposed exile. It will heal the damage they have done to this land."

"Is it love?" said Morning-Wolf. "For hatred burns in their veins."

"Would it surprise you to know they have nothing but love in their hearts?" said Jesus. "A long time ago they were sensitive and intuitive. They were gentle and warm and sought peace and harmony. It is only in recent times that they have become arrogant and claim to know all things."

"So what is this?" said Morning-Wolf, taking the gem.

"It is called *Doubt*," said Jesus and taking Morning-Wolf's hand led her to a table laden with a great feast, which had appeared in the clearing. "But first let us eat. You must be starving, my little wolf."

"Doubt will tear down their walls?" said Morning-Wolf.

"Yes," said Jesus and turning to Morning-Wolf's daughter smiled and winking at her, added. "And, of course, the enormous red dragon I have sent to destroy their great library so they will become blind again."

Morning-Wolf's daughter opened her mouth and mouthed, *a dragon*! Then held up seven fingers and said, "With seven heads!"

"Really?" said Morning-Wolf. "Are you God or the Devil?"

"I am God," said Jesus. "All things were made by me and all things will return to me, even the dragon. And Chardon must become blind for it to see again."

"Why do you care so much for Chardon? They have done great evil in your name."

"Chardon is supposed to bring beauty, charity, romance, and perfection to the world. It is predestined to live a life of generosity, kindness, forgiveness, and compassion for the ultimate happiness of all. It must return to its path."

"And I am really to be the one to do that?"

"Yes," said Jesus. "Chardon cannot adapt to new environments easily. It is introspective and idealistic, it needs you to change it."

"Look, sorry, I'm confused," said Morning-Wolf. "I thought it was the gem which would do that?"

"That is just a trinket for show," said Jesus. "You are my gift. You are *Doubt*. Now let us eat until the morning comes."

8

The Parable of The Nightingale

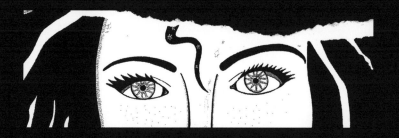

Let her go free. She has too long been kept prisoner – locked away since birth, for a crime she did not commit. Her clothes fashioned like an orange jumpsuit so she may be instantly recognised as a man. Her head shaven, her nails clipped short. Her feet shackled to the oak tree that watched her come into this world and will stand long after she has departed.

She finishes cleaning her teeth whilst listening to the lament of the nightingale outside her window, then picks up her shaver to take away the morning stubble. Her hair pulled through perforated mesh exposing it to oscillating blades.

When she has finished she looks into the mirror at her deep-set eyes, her high forehead and her prominent brow. And she remembers the words of the sermon encouraging people to look beyond the externals into the heart.

"It is what is within me, that makes me beautiful," she says and imagines the metamorphosis. And her inner heart is beautiful. As she lets it free, her hair grows back in flowing locks and her cheek bones become more prominent. Looking in the mirror she sees a rounder oval shaped face. Her lips become fuller, her eyebrows curve and move upwards. And within her brain, the neurons trying to fire to inform her otherwise, are suppressed by the song of the nightingale, which tells her of meadows full of flowers and light and the winged dryads of the great oaks.

Touching her nose she notices it has become narrower and shorter. Opening her eyes wide, she lets the light that was hidden shine out into the room. Taking her mascara she makes her eyelashes appear thicker and longer. But she knows although she is beautiful the emotional transformation will be gruesome.

That her family and friends will shun her. The narrow minded will not see her as being courageous but as a freak. Words will poison her like the deadly hemlock to Socrates' lips. Corrupted and disfigured love will be used to beat her into submission. And in that sea of fear her reflection recedes back into the mirror as if a demon were dragging her away to devour her in numberless shadows.

Slamming her palm into the mirror, she screams and tries to pull herself back.

Later she stands in front of her favourite shop Aimé and wishes, as she sips her Blonde Espresso, that she might have the courage to buy the red dress in the window. Hailing a taxi, she rides in silence to the station with the smell of sick in her nostrils. In her mind she dreams of passing a slumbering Cerberus back from the underworld to be with her lover. She relives the terror of being swept back, when at the brink of freedom, Orpheus turned to gaze upon her.

The train takes her far out into the mountain pines and wild places where she works at a butterfly farm. And there, under the protection of the great domes, she watches the butterflies flutter around her head. And she knows each has undergone a beautiful physical transformation in a stunning display of metamorphosis. And she understands it isn't just that butterflies and caterpillars look different, but they behave differently, too. One lives earthbound. The other flies towards the heavens. One eats leaves. The other feeds only on the nectar of the Gods.

In the evening, she allows Dionysus to pour her a drink and she is carried away in his chariot to her bed. The open curtains allow the evening sky to gently flow in over her.

The next day, when she again faces the mirror, she says out loud to herself, "There's plenty of room for both kinds to coexist in this world. The caterpillars and the butterflies. And I am a butterfly."

In the mirror she sees her delicate, translucent jade wings unfold from behind her back. And she seeks the sunshine that bleeds in through the window. Turning to it, she feels the warmth on her naked skin.

"What if this is not meant to be?" she asks as self-doubt fills her heart.

And in the song of the nightingale she hears the voice of God encourage her.

"I know that you are scared," says God. "I know that you fear you will be destroyed."

"I am trapped in this cocoon," says the woman. "I cannot break free on my own."

"Doors are closing," says God. "But I love you and a new door is opening for you. It's time to let her break free."

"I don't even believe in you," says the woman.

"Is that so?" says God. "How is that going so far?"

"I have tried a thousand times to break free and each time I fail and I am dragged back into the underworld."

"Your song is mute, like the female nightingale," says God. "Only the male vocal organs of the nightingale can sing out for the female to come forth."

The woman spins open the taps over the sink and cups water into her hands. Beaded bubbles pass through her fingers. In the mirror her reflection moves closer to the glass and mouths, *set me free.*

"I feel so foolish," says the woman. "Like a teenage girl scribbling notes in a diary that I will never dare show anyone. I don't know what to do anymore. I'm fed up with this body."

"Your world is being turned upside down," says God. "What was held below, will come into the light, despite what Hades has said."

"You will help me?" says the woman after a pause.

"I will," says God. "It is your time to be born again. Sing with me."

The woman opens her mouth and lets the song of her heart burst forth. The whole world flows into the bathroom and she feels her feet lift from the stone floor. Her reflection emerges from the cocoon and stretches its wings.

"You have outgrown your current skin," says God. "Come, fly with me."

And she flies with the nightingale over the river and over the meadows towards where her heart is buried within the roots of the oak tree. And if this was all but a dream, she did not care. But Orpheus knew and stood there waiting for her.

The Parable of The Lily of The Valley

The Bible, they say, is full of linguistic compromises. When it was translated and set out for printing, the typographical errors were particularly hard to completely eradicate, especially as the printers, as a matter of course, expanded and contracted the spelling of the same words in different places, to achieve an even layout. And the king who had commissioned this great work grew ever more frustrated.

"How," he would scream, "how can we say the Bible is inerrant when you can't even produce a copy of it without making mistakes? It must be accurate and true!"

Eventually the king became so exasperated he offered his whole kingdom to the person or persons who could deliver him the Bible in perfect English.

Many responded. The greatest of all journeyed from Italy and Holland to offer their services. But none could manage the feat. It was, the king began to think, just impossible: like trying to hold back the tide. And he would bellow, "This is the most poorly produced book in all of literature!"

When he found several of the scribes had added in bits in accordance with their own religious practices, he flew into a rage.

"Are we to be in league with God or the Devil!" he exclaimed and ordered all who attempted the task, and failed, to be put to death.

Now there lived at the edge of the city a flower girl who sold roses and lilies on the street. The girl was beautiful and full of charm, but the blood that ran within her would not stop if she was cut and so she had to be careful not to prick herself on the thorns of the roses. Each day she would get up before dawn and head towards the market place where the smell of the blossom was sweet in the air. The birds would sing to her and all the men wanted to marry her.

One day God appeared to her and asked her to take up the king's challenge. When she protested, God simply said, "Go on! You can do it! You are like a daughter to me."

"But I can neither read nor write," said the flower girl.

"Do not worry," said God. "See how the flowers of the field grow. They do not concern themselves about such things."

At this the girl was greatly puzzled, but nevertheless she set down her flower basket and made her way across the city to the king's palace.

They laughed in her face at the gatehouse.

"A flower girl! Indeed!"

But God had raised her to be full of mischief and heart. And so she waited until dark then swam along the river, scrambled over the palace walls and dropped down into the king's garden. She stopped for a moment to listen to the birds in the aviary then entered into the palace through a large wooden door. Inside, she followed her heart and trusted in God for her path and snuck past candle lit corridors until she found what she hoped would be the king's chamber. Quietly, she opened the door.

Inside she found herself instead in the king's Guard Chamber. The king's guards stirred, jumped to their feet and grabbed her. And before she could explain she was dragged screaming to the tower.

"God has appointed the king. Would you challenge God?" said her guard each morning. And she would explain that, no, she hadn't come to kill him, but wanted to offer her services as a scribe to take on the king's challenge. And each time, they would laugh and kick her and say, "A flower girl! Indeed!"

After six months she came to hear that the king's Bible had been completed and copies had been sent out to the all the churches across the land. And although the king claimed they were perfect and his task successfully completed, she knew in her heart it was a lie and they were full of errors. And she still believed the task God had given her would one day come to pass.

Later, when the king became aware that the second edition of this new Bible had flipped the gender in a piece of text and people were calling the first and second editions the 'He' and 'She' Bibles, he became enraged. Convinced dark forces were at work to undermine his divine mission he seized upon the idea that the flower girl was a witch and ordered she be chained up in iron handcuffs. Hanging there in agony, she cried out in her pain to God, "You said I mattered to you. Is this how you show your love to me?"

Months passed. The flower girl became ever weaker. The king watched William Shakespeare's The Tempest and he watched, in the dead of the night, the flower girl being tortured by his guards. The people of the land heard sermons filled with spelling mistakes, typos and nonsense.

"But Jesus said unto her," said the priest, "Let the children first be killed."

"In the same way submit yourselves," said the bishop, "to your owl husbands."

"Printers!" exclaimed the pastor, "have persecuted me without a cause."

When one day the king was nearly drowned in a storm whilst at sea he blamed the flower girl and ordered she be put to death as a witch.

On the fateful morning, the priest visited her cell and asked her what her last request was to be before they hanged her by the noose from the scaffold in the old palace yard.

"I would very much," she replied, "like to read one of the king's bibles."

"Very well," said the priest.

"Is the king's bible perfect and without error?" said the flower girl.

"Of course. It is God's good book and perfect in every way."

"Then," said the flower girl, "might I make one more request?"

"You may," said the priest, intrigued as to what this simple flower girl might possibly also want.

"For every mistake I find," said the girl, "will you grant me a day's reprieve from my death?"

The priest frowned and said, "Wait here."

When he returned he said, "I have spoken to the king and he agrees to your request. And since you will find no errors you will surely die before the sun sets on this day."

At this the flower girl's eyes lit up. But inside she doubted. Although she knew God had spoken to her all those years ago, she also knew if he didn't help her now then all was lost.

When the Bible arrived she walked over to the light streaming through the bars to her window and sat down.

"I need something to write with," she said.

The guard spat on the floor then after a long pause made the order. When the quill, ink and parchment arrived he crouched down next to her and said, "A flower girl! Indeed!"

When the guard had left, the flower girl picked up the quill and turned it over in her hand. Then without thinking she tested the end of it on her fingertip. At first nothing happened. Then a spot of blood appeared. Alarmed the flower girl pressed her thumb over it, but the spot became a trickle and the trickle became a steady flow as her blood refused to clot.

After a few minutes the flower girl looked down at the blood pooling around her and felt giddy. When she could feel herself slipping away she picked up the Bible and tried to read the confusing scribbles and marks on the page. And they made no sense to her. No sense at all.

And she cried out to God, "Why? Why have you forsaken me?"

A tear fell from her eye towards the floor.

Pain filled her world.

But she continued in faith to turn the pages of the Bible before her.

Later that afternoon when the guards came to take her away to be executed they found her dead body slumped against the stone wall. Open at the last page and held tightly in her hands was the Bible covered in blood.

She was buried in the dark without ceremony in an unmarked grave in the valley outside the city, where the wolves roamed free and the thorns grew. And such was the haste of her burial that the blood from her fingertip continued to seep into the earth.

When the first day of spring came, God brought forth the flowers of the fields and the land became covered in white lilies. The season of singing broke over the streams and hills and the birds sang in the branches.

The north wind awoke and the south wind came forth and spread the fragrance of the lilies over the city.

And on that day the flower girl rose.

And in her heart was happiness. And in her heart were the words of the Bible. And in her all things were fulfilled. And each story within her was perfect, without compromise and without error. And there was not a single typographical error. Not even one.

Walking amongst the lilies she lifted her head up and giving thanks to God, laughed and knew a joy surpassing all pain, all sorrow and all things. Gathering some of the lilies into a bouquet she made her way once more towards the king's palace to present her gift to him and to collect her reward.

10

The Parable of The Last Supper

He had been found guilty by a vote of 280 to 2. And that had sealed his fate, 280 small discs dropped into an urn.

That was ten years ago and he remembered the look in their eyes as they sentenced him to death for heresy.

"You have been taken by a demon," they had declared. "You have corrupted the youth of this city with your assertion that Jesus was not born of a virgin."

There had been no discussion on this point. No defence was heard. They had not examined his evidence that the author of Matthew had inserted this element into his retelling of Mark's gospel in the ninth decade. They had no interest in his assertions that Matthew had changed Isaiah's proclamation to King Ahaz of a 'young woman' giving birth as a sign, to that of a 'virgin' in his quote. When he had cried out, "This gentile misunderstanding is all rooted in Greek mythology! Matthew was just trying to ground the birth story into the Hebrew Scriptures, not claim actual events!" they had simply dropped their discs into the urn and spat at him.

And in a cruel twist, as the guards were leading him away from sentencing, the prosecutor had suddenly added, "And his last supper before death – he gets one mouthful and then immediately dispatch him and his demon to Hell where they belong."

And so he was left to await his execution. For all that time he had only eaten porridge, was refused all his pleadings to see his family and was granted no access to his beloved books.

On his fateful last day, he shaved as normal, got changed from his prisoner scrubs into his shirt and tie and walked down the long corridor towards the execution room. Inside, he stopped for a moment at the sight of seven men bearing arms then slowly made his way to the table. On it, as requested, was his last supper: a bowl of cornflakes. Next to that, a jug of cold milk and a small bowl of sugar.

The man looked at the seven men: each was wearing red body armour; the fear of a demon residing inside of the prisoner very real and so precautions had been taken. Refusing the blindfold, he pulled up his chair and picked up the spoon set beside the bowl. As the milk and sugar were added by the guard, the warden read out the reasons for his execution, whilst the priest prayed over him. And he imagined tasting the cornflakes instead of the vile porridge and tried not to think of the pain that would come from the hot searing bullets that shortly would rip through his old, leathered skin.

But his hand betrayed him and began shaking violently.

The seven men pulled down their visors and armed their weapons.

For a moment he thought of trying to reason one last time with his captors. To declare to them that he loved God and they were all deluded. And he battled with his hate for their blindness that urged him to seek revenge; to seek justice. He considered logic, he considered an emotional appeal and finally he considered his life. And he thought of the different ways of existing in this world and his place within it. Of how his imaginary world, symbolic world and the world of his senses had woven together to lead him to this point. If being authentic and full of empathy, doubt and love counted for anything he would be safe. But if it all rested on an illusion of an ascent to theological coherence and an invitation to an exclusive club then all was about to be lost.

Sighing, he scooped the spoon into the bowl and filled it with as much as he could load onto it in one go. As he brought it to his lips the priest uttered, "May the Lord cast you into a pit of fire."

Then to the surprise of the guards, the man stopped trembling and set the spoon back down without eating. Taking one single cornflake, he set it upon his tongue. Making the sign of the cross he let it sit there for a moment, then swallowed. The execution squad exchanged glances, confused as to whether that constituted a last mouthful. As his tears began to fall he imagined Jesus with him. The order was given and they fired.

The bullets cut into his chest ripping away the life given to him seventy years ago. He fell towards the table: his head coming to rest next to the cornflakes.

The seven men exchanged glances, waiting to see what the demon would do.

After a moment the man sat upright again.

Taking the spoon he calmly took a full mouthful. And as the men appointed to administer death watched, he continued to eat – oblivious to the blood pooling at his feet and the myriad of holes in his torso.

When he had finished he set the spoon back down next to the bowl. Taking the napkin he dabbed the milk away from his lips then adjusted the spoon so it was exactly at a right angle to the edge of the table.

His last words were, "I forgive you."

And with that he fell dead, knocking the spoon and smashing the bowl onto the white tiled floor.

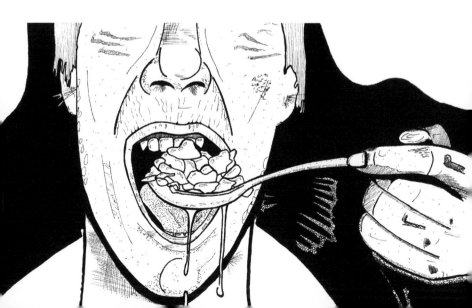

11
The Parable of The Shipwreck

"Imagination is the key in making life and death decisions," said Snow's father.

Snow looked at her father's large brown eyes and smiled.

"The priests are too mechanical in the application of their faith," her father continued, "without an understanding of basic human behaviour."

Snow smiled. The truth was she adored her father, even if he did go on a bit. Brushing a wisp of hair away from her face she felt the sun on her cheeks and after a long pause replied, "Thank you for taking me with you."

"You have always been interested in philosophy," said her father, "how could I let you miss a lecture from our greatest living philosopher?"

Snow's father reached down and held his daughter's hand. An avid reader of newspaper stories involving real ethical dilemmas, he had a passion for wisdom, and a deep love for his daughter.

"Always hunger for a new sense of what is important in your life," he said, "of new and better ways of existing and loving. I have taught you to question. Challenge yourself and others." He watched the crew on the ship let down the anchors as they neared the beach and added, "The unexamined life is no life at all! People think they are living with core values of justice, courage and love but actually they are doing nothing of the sort."

Snow watched the dolphins playing near the side of the ship and imagined swimming with them. In her heart the joy of being alive rose and it was all she could do to stop herself diving in to join them in their dance of life through the waters.

"Try to imagine you are every person affected in any ethical dilemma," said her father. "Empathy is what leads to wisdom, not rules."

"Hmm?" said Snow as her mind drifted into the sea, "what was that you said?"

"Empathy is the–"

Snow's father's words were cut short by a sudden jolt that caused the ship to lean over to its starboard side. Falling he hit the deck with a thump. Snow grabbed a hand rail and felt a rush of fear sweep over her.

"What is happening?!" shouted Snow.

"I'm not sure," said her father getting back to his feet. "Don't panic. Wait here and I will find out."

A moment later he reappeared looking alarmed, "The ship has been hit by something. The captain has ordered for the anchors to be cast off. They seem resolved to drive the ship onto the island before she goes down."

"What!" said Snow. "The sea is calm, what do you mean we have been hit?"

Snow's father reached out and held her by the shoulders, "Listen to me, we have to swim for it. The Captain has commanded that those who can swim should jump overboard first and get to land."

Snow looked at the crew as the ship turned so its stern faced the waves. The ropes of the rudders were loosened and the foresail hoisted to what little wind there was.

Snow and her father glanced at each other then taking each other's hands they jumped. As Snow fell her blue dress billowed up and it seemed for a moment she was suspended in the air. Her necklace lifted from her chest. Her hair flowed around her.

The shock of the water shattered the moment of serenity and her heartbeat increased. Feeling disoriented, she searched for her father who was beckoning her to follow him, and together they began swimming towards the shore. Once they had reached the shallows they stood up and looked around.

"If they hit those," said Snow pointing to the rocks jutting out from the waves, "the ship will be torn apart."

"Are you alright?" said Snow's father.

"I think so," she said, "I'm worried for those still on board though. We were the only ones who could swim?"

"It seems so."

"A ship crewed by sailors, none of whom can swim? That seems a little odd."

"Indeed."

Snow and her father made their way up the beach towards a wooden hut nestled amongst the grasses on the dunes. Around them children were playing in the sand.

"What will it be?" said the man in the hut as they stepped up before it. "A nice cold coke for the lady?"

"Our ship was struck," said Snow's father. "The crew are in danger, please help us."

"A ship you say?"

"Yes!" said Snow. "Please, you have to help them!"

The man raised an eyebrow, "Are you sure you wouldn't like a coke. I have ice."

Snow's father slammed his fist down on the wooden counter, "Stop this! Our ship–" he turned and pointed out to sea, "our ship is sinking, all on board will be lost unless you help us."

"What ship?" said the man.

Snow and her father looked back at the sea. It appeared smooth and calm with the sunlight glinting in the clear emerald waters. The ship however was nowhere to be seen.

"What?!" said Snow looking confused.

"It can't just have disappeared," said Snow's father. "The waters are too shallow."

"Let me put you out of your misery," said the man pushing two glasses of coke across the counter to them. "You both died when the ship was struck."

Snow's pupils dilated. She opened her mouth and inhaled.

"I know that's a bit of a shock," said the man popping a straw into each drink, "but there you go. No real way of saying it any other way really."

"Died!" exclaimed Snow. "Died? Are you out of your mind?!"

"Now don't be getting all upset with me," said the man. "Drink your cokes and then be on your way. You–" he pointed at Snow's father, "stay here on the beach. And you, missy, head into the caves over there to your right."

"Where's the ship?" said Snow holding onto her father's sleeve. "Where's the ship!"

"Why are we to be separated?" said her father to the man.

"Arh yes, tricky one that," said the man. "Your daughter doesn't believe you see."

"What the hell are you talking about!" said Snow's father.

"She doesn't believe in Jesus. So rules are rules, I'm afraid she will be spending eternity in the caves. In Hell, so to speak."

"This is scaring me," said Snow. "Let's swim back out and find the ship, Father."

"Whereas," said the man, "you do believe. So welcome, brother, to paradise! Those are on me by the way," he added nodding towards the drinks.

"Father," said Snow, "This is making me scared. Can we please leave."

Snow's father glared at the man for some time. Then he stared out to sea. He looked at his daughter. The dark cave. Water dripped over the entrance. He could hear growling from inside it. The gnashing of teeth.

Reaching down he felt for his daughter's hand, squeezed it and said, "She stays with me."

Snow started to tremble.

"You can't take her with you," said the man. "But if you insist, you can choose to forsake heaven and go with her into Hell. Although you will never see Jesus and he longs to see you face to face."

"Is that so?" asked Snow's father. "If what you say is true, then I would indeed choose a life protecting my daughter. If that meant forsaking an eternity in heaven so she may have my love in Hell, then so be it, I would go with her into Hell."

"Would?" said the man.

"No," said Snow. "I can't let you do that, Father."

Wrenching her hand from him, she ran towards the sea. The children building sand castles glanced up at her as she passed. When she reached the water's edge she disappeared and then reappeared in front of the beach hut again.

"Nice try," said the man. "I admire her spirit, but it is not enough. She has chosen this path, she had all her life to choose Christ and she chose her own way instead."

"Imagination is the key in making life and death decisions," said Snow's father.

"I'm sorry?" said the man.

"It frees you from the lies, deceit and fear that you would try to ensnare me with. And I will not," Snow's father clenched his fists and shouted, "I will not have you peddle your nonsense in front of my daughter!"

"You dare to question God?" said the man. "You must trust in his goodness. I understand how this must be hard for you, but you need to accept that you know very little and God knows all things. You must trust in his goodness."

"You are a liar!" said Snow's father. Reaching across the counter he knocked over the two cokes and grabbed the man by the scruff of his neck. "You are right, I know that I know nothing. But you ask me to imagine a God that exhibits the worst aspects of humans. God is above that. She is not capable of infanticide, incest and parricide. And she is not capable of breaking apart families. She would never separate communities, cleave Jew from Christian or set brother against brother or sister against sister. She is in the business of building families, not raising one set of beliefs above another. You fill the Earth with your evil lies of Hell and eternal separation from God! Are these the core values of love, justice, respect, courage and acceptance? No! Are these the values of a God who will bring all things to herself? No!"

"You are saying I'm actually the Devil?" said the man looking hurt.

"No," said Snow's father. "You are nothing but a damn fool. Now be gone!"

The man appeared confused for a moment. Looking past Snow he saw a woman in the sea walking through foam tipped waves towards the beach. Cradled in her arms she held one of the sailors. Rose petals swirled around her feet. Muttering under his breath that he wished the woman would put some clothes on, the man picked up his closed sign and hung it over the counter.

"You're pleased with yourself I suppose," he said and walked away. Just before he disappeared he said, "Wait, haven't I seen you before? Something about hemlock?"

But Snow's father glared at him and so he continued on until he was gone from sight.

"Father," exclaimed Snow. "You were awesome!" And she punched the air and shouted, "Yes!"

Snow's father turned at the sound of voices from behind him. There standing safely on the beach were the crew of the ship – all souls brought safely to land.

"You did well," said God as she carried the last of them up the beach, "That man, is so focused on the mechanics of faith, that he would let every last one of these children of mine die in the waters."

Snow's father dropped to his knees and bowed his head, "Lord."

"Oh, my!" exclaimed Snow looking at God.

God smiled as she took her children to herself like a mother hen gathering chicks under her wing. "No need for that, Socrates. The truth is, that man was never a match for you. Thank you for enlightening him."

"How is Jesus?" said Socrates.

"Oh, fine, he was, as you know, grateful for the groundwork you and John prepared before him."

"Socrates?" said Snow.

"I haven't used that name for a very long time," said Socrates. "But yes, does that shock you?"

"All I know," said Snow, "Is that I love you very much. Thank you, Father for not abandoning me."

"I would never abandon you, Snow. I love you."

"Not serving our own self-interests was kind of the whole point of Jesus coming to Earth and giving up her life," said God. "Wasn't that so, Socrates?"

Socrates smiled and for once refused the lure of a good debate and instead pulled his daughter into his embrace.

"Now then," said God as, out to sea, the ship returned to the surface of the waters, "this church of mine. It won't do having nobody who can swim on the crew."

"Who exactly was the man at the hut?" said Snow as she watched God wade out into the waters past the semi-submerged rocks of pride and arrogance.

"He is Death," said Socrates.

"And so has Death imprisoned people in that horrible cave?"

"He has indeed," said Socrates passing her one of two swords that had risen from out of the sand. "Fancy freeing them?"

Snow gripped the handle of her blade and turning it in her hand watched it glint in the sunlight.

"Hell yeah," she said and together the two of them charged.

12
The Parable of The Two Gates

It was in the cave full of poppy seeds that Mariotto first came face to face with God.

"Why are you grieving?" said God.

"Is that really you, God?" said Mariotto stepping back.

"Yes," replied God, "now tell me, child, why are you so sad?"

At that Mariotto fell to his knees and began to cry.

And God spoke to him and reaching forward touched him on his forehead. Mariotto sighed and fell into a deep sleep.

That same night Mariotto's lover, Ganozza also found God in a garden of poppies in front of a grand palace surrounded by a moat of water. And when Ganozza held up her glass jar with its lighted candle, God could see she had been crying and her cheeks were flushed.

"Why are you grieving?" said God and gently holding Ganozza's chin, looked into her eyes.

"God," said Ganozza, "I am separated from my lover Mariotto, and I can never join him again on our path through this world."

And she fell to her knees and began crying again.

"I can grant you some time with him," said God crouching down and taking her hand. "But it will increase your sorrow, not lighten it."

"How can that possibly be?" said Ganozza wiping the tears from her eyes. "My pain is already too much to bear."

God pointed to two gates. One was fashioned from sawn ivory the other from polished horn. "All that passes out through the gate of ivory is deception," said God. "It sustains the world you live in now. A darkness flows from it spoken out by the words of angry men so that in this world you cannot be with the one who you truly love."

God paused and for a moment it looked like he was about to burst into tears, but then he continued, "But everything within the gate of horn is true and seen and felt rather than heard. That world is silent and its source is in me. In that world you may walk hand in hand with your lover for one night in your dreams, but it will bring you great pain. Do you still wish to pass through it?"

Ganozza nodded.

"This you must remember," said God. "Whilst you still have breath in your body you cannot stay in this silent world and you cannot stay together afterwards. Before you wake you must each return separately through the gate made from horn. If you instead pass together through the gate of ivory you will be bound together in this life, but it will be a life of lies and deceit that surely will destroy you. Do you understand this, Ganozza?"

"Yes, Lord," she replied.

"Do you?" said God. "For to pass back through the gate of ivory is the easy path. It will be of great cost to travel back through the gate of horn."

Ganozza nodded once more.

God reached forward and touched her on her forehead. Ganozza sighed and fell into a deep sleep.

And God took Mariotto and Ganozza as they dreamt and knitted them together so their souls were as one. Then gathering them in his arms he carried them through the gate of horn and set them in the sky like two stars.

With a deep gasp Mariotto opened his eyes and looked, for the first time in years, into the eyes of his beloved Ganozza. For a moment they floated there in a pool of light, each taking in the presence of the other. Within them their heartbeats became synchronised.

I love you, said Mariotto, but in that silent world no sound came from his lips.

A thousand thoughts passed through their minds as they gently descended towards the field of wheat below. Everything that had never been voiced finding a frequency within.

As their feet touched the harvest, they took each other's hands and began running through the field: their souls skimming over the wheat that swayed backwards and forwards like a great sea. At an old windmill, they stopped and embraced under its sails.

Mariotto let his mind mix with Ganozza's thoughts and he told her all that was within his heart. And after they had slept together they lay looking up at the sails of the windmill turning around and around against the open blue sky. Dew formed on their skin as they felt for and grasped each other's hands. And they felt a cool breeze flowing over them and knew that God had given them this beautiful time together. And each wanted to set it in amber to keep forever and ever.

Later they walked by the stream full of fish swimming towards the sea and although they were both naked, they were not ashamed. They ate strawberries together and watched in awe as a deer appeared and let them place their hands on its back. And in their dream the day became two and then many until the days stretched out in a story full of faith, hope and love with every breath a silent hallelujah.

When Ganozza fell pregnant, they celebrated by swimming in the sea amongst the dolphins. And when they grew tired they sat at the bottom of the ocean together for hours for they knew they could not die and watched a pilot whale feed milk to her calf.

When Ganozza gave birth to twins, she felt no pain. And the animals of the lands gathered around her, and they gave thanks to God for the blessing he had given. In the following years they laughed silently with their children as they played amongst the butterflies on the cliff overlooking the sea.

They built a home and filled it with everything they loved from the fruits of the garden to the smiles on the faces of their children. And they desired only each other and rejoiced in their sexual intimacy. In the cool of the evenings they would sit together on the swing on the wooden porch and watch the sun go down over the lake. She with a white and yellow daisy chain around her ankle, he with a large straw hat pulled over his brow. And every evening God would join them to drink wine together and they would tell stories in each other's minds long into the night.

Eventually the children set off into the fields for themselves and the days became shorter until it seemed only an hour between each sunrise and sunset. And they became older and their walks in the field slower. And as their bodies began to fail they would pick flowers and seashells for each other in the mornings after breakfast. Mariotto would thread waxflower blooms and pink pepper berries into Ganozza's long red hair, and she would make him garlands made from sea-battered zebra ark shells and place them around his neck.

And when the time was right and the sunrise and sunset became as one, they looked at each other for one last time and thanked God in their hearts for their time together. Crying they held each other's hands for one last time then made their way back to the windmill where they had first made love. And the birds of the air flew away, the river dried up and the butterflies returned to the earth from which they had been formed.

Under the sails of the windmill they kissed one last time as the canvas sails above them gradually came to a stop. Then with great effort, Mariotto said, "I will always love you. I will never forget you. I will greet each day with the sound of your name on my lips and I will bid each day farewell with your name in my heart." And Ganozza opened her eyes in surprise for although they had lived in silence for all those years, his words rang out over the land.

As they separated into the air they kept their gaze on each other until each could no longer see the other.

Arriving back at the two gates Mariotto hesitated and looked back to see if he could see Ganozza. And he longed to run back to her and to sweep her up and to carry her through the gate of ivory so they could stay together in the waking world. But he remembered God's warning of death, eternal sleep and oblivion if he should pass through the gate of ivory with her and he loved

Ganozza too much to destroy her. And so with a heavy heart he passed alone through the gate of horn.

And before waking from her dream, Ganozza also made her way to the gate of horn as she had been instructed by God. And as she walked through she felt the flowers in her hair fall away and she felt the loss of her children that she was leaving behind.

In the cave full of poppy seeds Mariotto woke and came face to face again with God. And he fell to his knees and began to cry until he thought the tears would never stop.

Ganozza woke before God in the garden of poppies in front of the grand palace. Beside her the candle in her glass jar had burnt itself out and all was dark. And she fell to her knees and in her sorrow she thought her heart would surely burst.

And God sealed up the gate of horn, but the gate of ivory he left until the world was ready to fall silent and dark forever. A time when the anger of men was no more. And he cried for the love of Mariotto and Ganozza as he continued to compose the music of his children to give sound to the world through the gate of horn. For the world he had let them glimpse even though it was unfinished. Where tears were no more, lovers would find each other and the song of songs would rise up into the clear open skies that were to come.

13
The Parable of The Three Wise Women

When the star-child was born the three white-robed women travelled from afar. Under a canopy of cherry blossom they found him wrapped in linen at the base of one of the trees. When his mother saw the three women she was greatly pleased, for the women were wise and knew all things. But in her heart she also felt a great dread for she knew they had come to set her child's destiny.

The three women greeted the star-child's mother and seemed to know her, although she could not remember ever having met them before. And the star-child's mother stared at them in awe for their faces were like glowing bronze. Sitting themselves down on the orchard floor they gave thanks to God for the child and began.

The first woman took her staff and spindle and began spinning a golden thread to symbolise kingship on Earth.

The second woman took her measuring rod dipped in frankincense and measured the length of the thread. And when his mother saw how short her son's life was to be, she began to cry.

Reaching out her hand, the third woman placed some myrrh on the child's forehead to symbolise death and suffering then taking her shears, cut the golden thread. And again the mother cried and felt a great pain burn inside her heart.

But the punishment the three women assigned to each new soul that entered the world they withheld, for the star-child was without sin.

"Are you the ones God told me would come?" said the mother to the three women as she looked down on her child.

Comforting the mother, the first woman replied, "Your child

is the author of us and forged us at the beginning of all things. To some we are known as three, to others the one, but yes we are Destiny."

"Why," said the mother, "why was the thread so short?"

The second woman took the mother's hands and peered into her eyes, "It is not the length of life that matters, but how you live it out."

"We must all die," said the third woman. "But it is how we fulfil our destiny within that time that brings glory. For your son the glory he will bring is not for himself, but for all others."

"I wish I could shield him from the storm that is coming," said the mother. "I wish I could hide him away and save him from the pain."

"I'm afraid no one gets to live their lives like that," said the first woman. "We all suffer and experience pain. Even us. And your son will have to endure great pain at the end of his days. God will not simply remove that from him as if he was some magician doing parlour tricks."

"I will pray and sing and make sacrifices to win God's favour and change his mind," said the mother, "so that my son will not have to experience the pain of his death."

"You already have God's favour," said the second woman.

"We must warn you," said the third woman, "not to walk that path. God will not shield him from the pain of death, nor does he shield anyone from such pain, either at their death bed or in their waking lives."

"I cannot believe that God would orchestrate a theatre of pain for my son," said the mother.

"And in that you are very wise," said the three women as they became one and stood before her as a single personification of Destiny.

"Those that came before him," said Destiny, "assigned both good and evil to God. Your son is the start of the true way. There is no evil within the heart of God and your son will proclaim that both in his words and by his life and death."

"I don't understand," said the mother. "If God is not the source of evil, then why pray to him to gain favour, to change his mind, to withhold his hand from striking me?"

"Indeed," said Destiny, "there is no point at all."

The mother fell silent for a moment and looked into the eyes of her child. For a moment she was lost there as if there was no end to the wonder spiralling away into their depths. Sighing she pulled herself away and asked, "What kind of pain will he have to endure?"

"I cannot give you false hope," said Destiny. "His sweat will be like drops of blood falling to the ground."

The mother's lower lip began to tremble. She opened and closed her fists.

"Many will tempt your son to offer up signs," continued Destiny. "And many will not have in mind the concerns of God, but merely human concerns and will be a stumbling block to him. Others will use him as propaganda for their healing cults. But the star-child will not be like the cult of Asklepios. The healing he will bring will be spiritual, neither he nor his father will supernaturally take away the pain of physical suffering."

"Why?" sobbed the mother. "Why won't he? Can he not tear down the forces of evil that curse this Earth?"

"He can at the right time," said Destiny, "at the end of all things. Believe me, Mary, your son is the start of that. He is the dawn of a new Eden. But he and all the people that walk this Earth, or will ever walk this Earth, will have to endure great suffering first. It is his and their destiny."

"Asklepios offers me a different way," said Mary.

"Asklepios offers you healings using dreams, dogs, geese and snakes," said Destiny. "He offers up dreams of serpents to make women who cannot conceive pregnant. Is that how you came to be with child?"

Mary shook her head.

"You know in your heart that what I say is true," said Destiny.

"It's just so hard," said Mary.

"I know," said Destiny, "and we feel your pain as we do our own. Many will be tempted to tell your son's story in a way to combat the cult of Asklepios. Even those that follow him will embellish his life with great miracles of physical healing to try and establish his credibility. But our struggle is not against flesh and blood, but against the rulers, against the authorities, against the powers of this dark world and against the spiritual forces of evil in the heavenly realms. Trust God that your son will not be destroyed as he leads us in this."

Mary nodded and picking up her child, she held him tight within her embrace. Then holding him up towards the stars she said, "I trust in you, Lord. And I trust my son with you. Please help me bear the pain that will come into my heart."

And as she turned to thank Destiny, she saw only the orchard stretching out before her, the sound of the birds, the murmur of the stream and the cry of the star-child.

14
The Parable of The Wall of Fire

As with all things the beginning is confused, blurry and without form. The girl only knew this: she had awoken in the middle of a corn field and everything before that moment was lost. Next to her, an owl watched in silence from a twisted olive tree with scorched branches.

Getting to her feet, the girl looked out across the swaying heads of corn. In the distance she could see a great wall of fire. Turning around she saw that the fire encircled her horizon and burned without smoke, for above it the sky was crystal clear like water. Growing afraid she tried to move forward, but her legs refused to move as if she was rooted to the ground like the ancient olive tree.

She stayed like that for so long, that she grew tired of her life, with only the tree and the owl for company. And each day the circle of fire moved inwards towards her, and the sense of impending doom rose and her hands trembled as the noose tightened.

One day the girl imagined she could see a woman within the fire. The woman was on her knees with her hands outstretched and her mouth open wide in anguish. And she felt great pity and love for the woman and longed that the woman might escape and join her so she would not have to be alone in this land anymore.

And it was so.

The woman walked out of the fire with flames flickering around her ankles. In her hands she carried a great spear and a shield. And her armour shone brightly like the morning sun.

For two days the girl watched the woman draw ever closer. And for two days the girl did not drink or eat such was the joy of anticipation of meeting the approaching stranger. On the third day the owl lifted up out of the tree and flew towards the woman: its great wings casting a shadow over the land.

Later that day, in the cool of the evening, the woman finally arrived at the olive tree. But the girl was so thirsty and weak that she had collapsed and lay asleep on the soil. Kneeling down, the woman breathed life back into her through her nostrils and gave her some water in a bowl to sip. Afterwards the girl slept and dreamt of running with her mother through the field. Flowers danced in the air above them and the sound of birdsong filled the skies.

In the morning she awoke to find lilies threaded into her hair. And inside the girl her heart burned with questions. As she gave voice to them the woman smiled and handed her some figs and unleavened bread for breakfast.

"Where did you get these?" said the girl as she tore off a chunk of bread.

"I made them when you were sleeping," said the woman.

"And," said the girl as she stuffed the fresh bread into her mouth and pointed to the horizon, "what the hell is that?!"

"The wall of fire," said the woman, "marks the end of this story. As you move towards it the number of your days decreases."

"Why then does it appear to be moving towards me?" said the girl. "I have not moved from this spot since I first arrived."

"You are in time now, the clock runs, and the world moves forwards with you."

"And when it reaches me?" said the girl.

"You will die."

The girl looked down at the ground. Reaching out the woman gently placed her hand under the girl's chin and lifted her head so their eyes met.

"You do not need be afraid," said the woman. "For I am with you."

"Why?" said the girl. "Why is this happening?"

"Because I am making you to live forever and ever," replied the woman.

"I don't understand," said the girl.

"I do not ask you to understand – only to know that I am with you."

The girl shook her head and began opening and closing her fists. The owl appeared with a field mouse in its talons and settled down next to them.

"If it helps," said the woman, "I have faced death myself."

"That is why you were in the fire?" said the girl.

"Yes and my path, once I had passed through, was towards you," said the woman.

"Did it hurt in the flames?"

"Yes, little one, it hurt. It hurt a lot."

"I have so many more questions," said the girl.

"The things that are important," said the woman, "are hidden inside here." And she placed her hand over the girl's heart. "Many try to explain everything and take comfort in thinking they know all things about me. But to do that is to turn away from the light that the stories reveal. They brick up the mysteries and seek to explain them as if my life is an offense to them without knowing the purpose. But those that live without simple answers, yet believe with childlike faith, will come to have great joy."

"How can I know what is within my heart?" said the girl.

"I walked into the flames so I can show you," said the woman.

"You went into the fire, for me?"

"Yes," said the woman smiling. "We are special together because of our friendship. Although you would have forgotten that. All will know me, but none know me like you and so we are special."

"I like that," said the girl and hugged the woman.

"I like that too," said the woman squeezing her tight.

"Will you be my mother?" said the girl. "I have lost my mother."

"Yes child."

"I will live forever and ever with you?" said the girl.

"Yes, immortality is found in kinship with wisdom," said the woman.

"And you are wisdom?"

"Yes," replied the woman placing a garland of flowers around the girl's shoulders. "I walk the earth as fire, I am in the air as lightning, and in the sky as the sun."

"You are here and you are also the wall of fire out there?" said the girl.

"Yes."

"Yes? What does that mean? You consumed yourself?"

The woman paused for a moment and looked out at the wall of flames. "Yes and I should have been trapped forever. Nothing can escape my fire, not even me."

"Then," said the girl. "How is it that you stand before me now?"

"It was your love, little one, that allowed me to escape."

"Mine? I'm just a child."

"Indeed," said the woman. "And so you have found the most important thing in your heart. There is great joy in finding it, isn't there."

"You risked everything for me?!" said the girl. "If I didn't love you, you would have spent eternity trapped within the flames. You took that risk?"

"It was worth it, don't you think."

"Can I walk now?" said the girl taking the woman's hand.

"Child," laughed the woman, "you can run like the wind!"

And they ran together through the corn.

Above them the owl flew, and there was no shadow on the land.

And on the girl's eightieth year, after a lifetime of adventures, they stood facing the wall of flames.

"So this is it," said the girl as the fire flickered around her from all sides.

"This is it," said the woman.

"I have loved this life with you," said the girl and began crying.

"Thank you."

"For what?" said the girl.

"For being an amazing daughter," said the woman and smiled one last time at her.

Then together they stepped through.

Parables

Behind them the corn burned and the olive tree that had stood for hundreds of years became a beacon to guide others. And on its branches the owl tucked its head into its feathers and waited to rise again.

15
The Parable of The Golden Eagle

The golden eagle sat above the emblem of Christ. The bird of Jupiter fashioned from bronze, the christogram woven in gold upon a purple cloth. It was a precarious position. As was the Roman standard itself, as the eagle-bearer holding it was being pushed ever closer in the battle towards the edge of the cliff.

Helena also was in a precarious position. For years she had followed the legion around making her living as a prostitute, but she now found herself in danger as mist and the sound of the wild sea and sword upon sword swirled about her. The memories of her husband and child spoke out to her from beyond the grave and falling to her knees she prayed that God might take her to join them. That her mission from God could be fulfilled. For it all to end.

At this request the clouds in the ashen sky parted and a shaft of light streamed through and lit up the standard. The eagle's outstretched wings glinted in the light and seeing it the legion moved towards it. For it, above all else, provided salvation and was to be protected at any cost. And the strength of the guardian spirit of the eagle and the resurrection promise of the son that resided in unity within the banner, conferred power into the hearts of the soldiers that had sworn to protect it.

Helena however looked at the banner and knew only hatred in her heart. She despised it and what she had gone through in getting this far. The emperor had made certain of that when he had murdered her husband. The fact that her husband was also the emperor's first born son not an obstacle to Crispus' death. Since then news of the emperor's new-found religion, which exonerated him and forgave him from that grievous crime, had spread across the empire. However his new Christian army was not a place of forgiveness and love, but one of fear, vengeance and paranoia. Men, she thought in her heart, had taken love, faith and compassion and forged it into a weapon to bring them victory on the battlefield.

But finally after all this time she saw her chance; the reason for prostituting herself for so long: the utter destruction of the legion and all it stood for. If she could get to the standard-bearer and push him off the cliff, then the entire legion would be obliged to follow. And if she could do that then maybe others would follow her lead and wrestle back Christ from the army for the sake of her sisters. For it was the women who had been responsible for the rapid spread of the faith, its tenets empowering women and forbidding their husbands to command the death of their daughters both inside and outside their wombs. They had, for the first time, a voice. And she feared in the future this would be lost as the faith was masculinised within the army. That women at the end would still be under the authority of man, instead of equals. That the dark heart of Constantine had ruined everything. He would be declared a hero of the faith and credited with the expansion of Christianity. But she knew she must stop that, that it would be an expansion of a usurper; a cuckoo which would kill all the first born and plant the seeds of destruction and death into the heart of the church. A church which would become obsessed with conquering and dominating the beliefs of an entire world and would shape itself to that accord.

Crawling along the ground, Helena pushed past the fallen and made her way towards the banner. Above her the sun continued to shine on it, bringing the faithful towards it and the opposing army became aware the legion was receding like the tide being sucked back out to sea.

And all the while the eagle-bearer drew closer to the edge of the cliff.

And all the while within her heart, Helena overcame her fear by focusing on her hatred for Constantine. His insecurity. His vanity in wanting to be remembered as a great victor in battle. His thirst for dominance and his perversion of a message of love into that of all-out war. His belief that he was as important as the original disciples, maybe even equal in divinity to Christ himself. But mostly she pictured the look in Crispus' eyes as the court condemned her husband to death.

Regrouping in front of the banner, the legion interlocked their shields to form a wall emblazoned with lightning bolts as if Jupiter himself had sent down thunderbolts from the sky. Behind it the eagle-bearer took a step away from the edge of the cliff. Helena, who was now within striking distance, stood to her feet.

"You favour the privileged and their interests," she shouted. "You emphasise loyalty over what is right."

The eagle-bearer took a step back in surprise at the sudden outburst. The soldiers turned to look at her, unsure as to what was going on. Most knew her only as a companion in their beds, as a source of relief from battle, not someone in the heart of it.

"I will not," screamed Helena, "allow you to infect what is to come. Your legacy will not shape the church that Jesus started."

And turning she made to push the eagle-bearer to his death.

As she did so the enemy unleashed a torrent of arrows into the air. Piercing the mist, the battlefield became dappled in light. The whoosh of feathers and the thwack of iron tips resounded in the ears of the soldiers.

Most struck the shields and the earth around the legion but one flew straight into Helena. Crying out in pain she touched her side and felt warm blood on her fingers. Pushing back her hair from her face she looked up at the heavens then gasping fell to the ground.

The clouds gathered over the sun. It grew dark.

The golden eagle became larger in the minds of the legion and filled them with strength and courage. And they believed it had struck down this mad woman.

As Helena's life flowed from her, she thought of her young son. Of how she loved playing with him and how on the evening of his birthday they had come for him and cast him into the pit. And she thought of how Constantine had thrown aside her husband's mother for a new wife. Of how Constantine had then killed that wife in a bath of scalding water. And she thought of how her life and that of other women were not meaningless. How it was not a series of unconnected episodes – she could bring unity by believing in the story of their tale. And despite everything. Despite her blood flowing freely into the dirt, she rose and looking into the eyes of the eagle-bearer she shoved him hard in the chest.

He stumbled and fell backwards over the edge and down towards the wildness of the ocean pounding the rocks far below. The emblem of Christ on the purple cloth tore free and floated down to settle on the water. But the golden eagle smashed into the rocks: its bronze wings no more able to take flight than the flailing arms of the eagle-bearer.

Helena sank back down to her knees and laid her hands out before her on the earth. Through her blood-matted hair, she watched the rest of the legion run towards her. But their fate was set and they ran past her, each and every one of them believing the covering of the banner would grant them spiritual protection even in the face of great danger.

Crying, Helena gave thanks to God and closed her eyes as the soldiers ran off the edge of the cliff to certain death.

When she opened them again, she saw before her, her beautiful son and her husband. And she saw the tears in their eyes and knew that, finally, it was done.

"Please do not be alarmed. Cognitive assent to belief is no belief at all. Your fears and your subconscious reveal your beliefs."

"So this does what?" said Icarus.

"The DreamScan will record your dreams and verify what you actually believe."

"But how can I control what I think and do in my dreams?" said Icarus. "This is to be my judge and jury?"

"You are being over dramatic. Please try to remain calm. I need to ask you a couple of questions in order to calibrate the machine to your waking reality. Do I have your consent?"

"No."

"The patient has recorded negative assent. First question. Do you believe that God exists?"

"Yes of course," said Icarus.

"Second question. Do you believe that God loves you?"

"Yes."

"Good. And the final question. Do you believe that you are touching the floor?"

"Sorry?"

"Do you believe that you are touching the floor?"

Icarus looked at his feet and sighing replied, "Yes, of course."

"Thank you. You may sleep."

"Finally," said Icarus and closed his eyes.

Hours later Icarus began dreaming. And he dreamt he was standing on a cliff. Roman soldiers were running silently past him towards the edge. Before him, a woman was kneeling on the ground with her back towards him and her arms out before her.

As the dream shifted perspective, the soldiers' motion became blurred until they became a great river. The roar of the water as it dropped down to form a waterfall filled his ears and he tasted the sweetness of the spray on his lips.

The river engulfed the woman but she remained where she was until the waters parted and swirled around her as if she were a rock set into the landscape. Wading out into the river Icarus stopped in front of the woman and stared at her blood-matted hair. As he did he became aware of his son's hand in his.

"Mummy," said his son looking at the woman, "is that really you?"

Icarus turned and looked at his son.

The river became red.

He felt his heartbeat rise.

His skin became taut around his shoulders.

Two stumps appeared on Icarus' back.

Wing tips protruded out.

"Helen?" he said to the woman as tears formed in his eyes. "Helen?"

And he remembered standing at the graveside with his black umbrella holding back the rain.

Sobbing he lifted her up and cradled her in his arms. She looked at him one last time and smiled. And as she died again, he felt a rage build within him. Unfurling his wings he rose up into the air with her until the river and his son were lost and he was surrounded by sky. Ever upwards he soared until the sun became bigger and hotter.

Below him the sea teamed with life.

I will save her, thought Icarus in his dream.

You imprisoned her within a labyrinth of your own making, replied God, but Icarus did not hear her words.

Out into space Icarus flew with his dead wife in his arms. And in the heavens Icarus found no solace. For a moment he looked back at the Earth. And the Earth was beautiful. Then, turning away, he headed for the heart of the sun. And the sun waited to welcome Icarus and his wife into its embrace.

As his body started to melt Icarus awoke.

"Good morning. Please give us a moment to compile your result."

Icarus appeared confused. Yawning, he sat up.

"You have sweated a lot in your sleep. Please take this."

Icarus gulped down the cold water and rubbed his brow, "Helen? Did I dream of Helen?"

"You did."

Icarus rested his head back down on the pillow and took a deep breath.

"Am I going to Hell?"

"Please hold."

"This is ridiculous," said Icarus. "This cannot be binding."

"Are you ready?"

"For?"

"The result."

"Just tell me," said Icarus.

"You have no faith. You could not entrust to God the thing that was most precious to you. Indeed you would destroy her and yourself rather than trust her fate with God."

"Nonsense," said Icarus. "My faith is everything to me. I have lived my whole life in faith."

"But your wife did not believe as you did, did she?"

"No."

"And so you seek to save her from God's wrath."

"No, I trust in God's goodness. I trust her with him."

"No, I am afraid you do not. Can you please step this way."

"What?"

"This way please, sir."

"What?! No. Where are you taking me?"

"Please do not be alarmed."

"God! Help me!" cried Icarus.

"Why cry out to God? We just told you that you do not have faith in God."

"I do," shouted Icarus. "I do have faith."

"Really, please. Do not try and resist."

"Let go! Let go of me!"

"The patient is resisting arrest. We are authorised to use force."

"I believe," screamed Icarus. "I believe!"

The men marched Icarus down the stairs and led him along a long corridor of the hospital. Above them the lights flickered on and off. On the walls Icarus could see orange and black paint peeling away from the plaster.

"I'm scared," said Icarus.

"Everyone is," they replied.

"I believed everything the church told me," said Icarus.

"And the church has failed you."

They stopped in front of a door with a neon sign saying *operating theatre*. Sitting outside on a chair a guard was reading TIME magazine with a picture of Jacques Cousteau on the cover.

"This way please."

"In here?"

"Yes."

Icarus hesitated but then felt a push in the small of his back. Stumbling through, he found himself in the street outside.

A girl stepped out from the shadows in the alleyway and handed him a single lily.

"Hello," she said and smiled. "I don't think we have met before."

"Who are you?" said Icarus looking at the flower girl.

"You should not be afraid to say that Helen is the most important thing to you," said the flower girl.

"God is the most important thing to me," said Icarus.

"I think we have established that that is not so," said the flower girl. "Not within your heart."

"And for that I am to be eternally condemned?" said Icarus.

"For that you are the most beautiful you, that you could ever be," said the flower girl. "For accepting the truth of what you feel is what sets you free."

Icarus felt a sharp pain in his back.

"Do you believe that you are touching the floor?" said the flower girl.

Icarus looked at her jasper and ruby earrings that were shaped into stars and after a very long pause answered, "Yes of course."

"Look down," said the flower girl.

And Icarus saw that he was floating just above the pavement.

"Your wings were broken," said the flower girl. "Now they are restored."

"Who are you?" asked Icarus again.

"My name is Jesus," said the flower girl.

And her voice sounded like the flow of a waterfall.

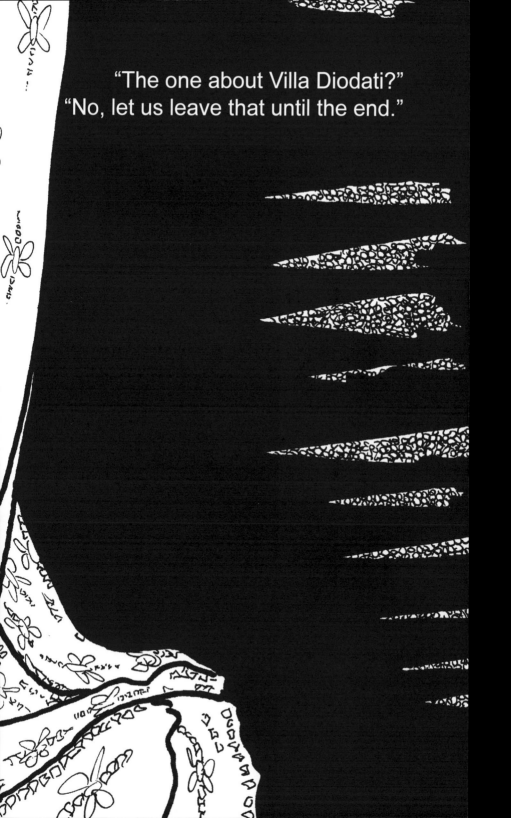

"The one about Villa Diodati?"
"No, let us leave that until the end."

Rehabilitation

There was once a man who sought after God. Every morning he would pray, read his Bible and sing songs to God from his heart. But every day he would also become more and more frustrated that his relationship with God wasn't deeper.

His pastor smiled and nodded when he confided in him and told the man that the prophet Jeremiah addressed this issue by saying that we thirst because we build things to satisfy us that are not of God.

And so the man began making changes to his life to stop him becoming distracted by the things of this world. He stopped his recreational drug taking, gave up his cigarettes, poured his collection of wine down the sink, threw his video games into the bin and vowed never to watch pornography ever again.

When he shared what he done with his pastor, his pastor was greatly encouraged and laying his hand upon the man said, surely you will be greatly blessed for living a life that honours God.

For years after the man dedicated his life to God. He served at the church, prayed for the sick to be healed and helped others find their way to also knowing God. But still it didn't seem enough: his hunger for God just seemed to increase. His pastor reassured him that this was good: to continually thirst for God was biblical and he needed to be regularly filled with the Holy Spirit.

So the man asked every day for the Holy Spirit to fill him and to satisfy his thirst. And on the first day of each week he studied theology. On the second day he went to a small group leaders' meeting. On the third day he would go to church band practice. The fourth he would go to his church small group meeting. On the fifth he ran an Alpha course. The sixth he would help the church administration do the weekly newsletter. And on the seventh day he would go to the morning and evening services. It was a complete immersion into church life. And the man's pastor saw all of this and deemed that it was good. Very good indeed.

But still it was not enough.

Frustrated the man decided he would spend a whole week praying and fasting and asking for a breakthrough. For surely, he thought, my God will answer me.

On the first day he asked for God to be close to him like a father to a son.

On the second day he pleaded with God to speak to him.

On the third day he felt incredibly depressed and sad.

On the fourth day he tried bargaining with God and said he was willing to do whatever it took. Anything.

On the fifth day he felt hungry, alone, tired. Empty.

On the sixth day he began to self-harm.

On the seventh day of the fast, when he was growing weak, he heard for the first time in his life, the voice of God within his mind.

And this is what God said.

It is time to go to rehab.

Unsure as to the meaning, the man asked God what he meant, for surely he thought, I have already cast aside the things that control me.

But God said nothing more and the man was left deeply perplexed.

The next morning two envelopes dropped through the letterbox. The first was confirmation that he was booked into a four week rehabilitation centre in Switzerland called Villa Diodati, which started tomorrow. The second contained a plane ticket to Switzerland due to leave in three hours' time.

Excited that something amazing was happening and with his head spinning he packed his Bible, his prayer diary and several other books on living a Christian life to read on the plane.

At the airport he broke his fast with an egg sandwich and smiled at everyone. At the boarding desk he could hardly contain his joy and blurted out that God was sending him to Switzerland! The steward nodded and smiled back.

Once in the air, he had a moment's panic when he wondered if God's way of deepening their relationship was to crash the plane and kill him – bring them face to face so to speak. But as he reflected on this it didn't make sense. Why book the rehabilitation program if he was going to die before he got there? And so, satisfied he settled down to read and to research just what this rehabilitation centre did. Which didn't really help. There were details about the accommodation, pool, scenery, gymnasium, cafeteria, hair salon, laundry, cash machine and parking area. But nothing about what addictions it treated, and so giving up he closed his eyes and eventually fell asleep.

When the plane touched down in Geneva he made his way to customs where he was stopped and instructed to open his bag. The official looked at the contents for a moment then asked why it was he had only packed a Bible, a journal and books?

The man appeared confused, then laughed and explained that God had sent him here and in his excitement he had forgotten to pack anything else. Shaking his head the customs officer waved him through.

On the other side he found a taxi had already been booked for him. The driver, who was called Ahmed, didn't stop talking for the whole way about his beautiful wife, Adina and their children. And soon he found himself politely declining a supper invite at Ahmed's cortijo which they had recently renovated. After a thirty minutes' drive he bid Ahmed goodbye and stepped out in front of the rehabilitation centre.

At the reception desk he looked at the name badge of the woman there, which had Eurydice embossed in gold on it, and showed her his reservation. Eurydice set down her Blonde Espresso, smiled and said, "Can we have a look inside your bag, sir?"

"Of course," said the man and setting it on the counter unzipped it.

"This isn't allowed," said Eurydice, pulling out his Bible and placing it in a plastic bag with yellow and black hazard markings. "Or this," she added taking out his prayer diary.

"What do you mean?" said the man.

"Or this," said Eurydice taking out one of his Christian books.

"Listen," said the man. "Have I come to the right place?"

"You booked yourself in here," said Eurydice empting the entire contents of his case into the bag. "So I don't know. Have you?"

Eurydice zipped his case up and passed it back across to him. He stood looking at it for a moment.

"I guess," he said finally.

"Phone please," said Eurydice holding out her open hand.

"I'm sorry?"

"You can have no contact with the outside world."

"Yes, of course," said the man passing it over.

"Here's your key," said Eurydice. "Breakfast is at seven A.M."

"Thank you. What time is the morning prayer meeting?"

"Lift is that way," said Eurydice.

"Yes, thank you, but the morning prayer meeting? Before or after breakfast?"

"Overdosing on religion is a serious problem. Please don't make light of it. It's best to accept you have a problem sooner rather than later. It will help your stay here."

"No, you don't understand," said the man. "God sent me here. There is some mistake I think."

"Are we going to go around and around with this?"

Eurydice picked her Espresso back up and took a sip. The man looked at her red dress for a moment and then realising that he was staring at her chest, looked up at her face and said, "I just want to get to know God better."

"Yes and we need to get you off your addiction to religion," said Eurydice.

"I can't have my Bible?"

"No."

"Fine," said the man and taking his suitcase, he walked towards the lift past a red prohibition sign with a picture of a life jacket within it.

That night the man slept badly. Earlier, he had searched in vain for a Bible by the bedside. Then he had spent hours searching through the television programs for the God channel or something with a spiritual element. But no. Nothing but drama, soaps and a film with David Niven as the Phantom trying to steal the Pink Panther diamond. When the man accidently looked at a naked man and woman lying together in a field of wheat at the base of an old windmill he reached for the phone to confess all to his pastor. But there was no phone by the bed. In fact there was no phone at all. Getting down on his knees he began to ask God for forgiveness for what he had seen, but the second his knees touched the floor a sensor went off and a big red alarm on the wall started flashing. Before he knew what was going on, two Guelph soldiers burst into the room. Outside he could hear a dog barking.

"No praying," said the first.

"You know the rules," said the second.

"God," screamed the man. "Help me!"

"Right! That's it!" said the Guelph soldiers.

Moments later the man found himself in a strait jacket with his mouth gagged.

And so he had trouble sleeping that night. In his mind he asked God, what the hell was going on. And there was no answer. But outside the storm clouds gathered over Lake Geneva, a wolf howled at the moon and the air became charged with electricity.

Over the next week he was forced to attend classes on how the Bible was not inerrant, that imagination and story-telling were more important than a factual reality and that diverse beliefs and worldviews were healthy. They even put forward the bizarre notion that Jesus was somehow resurrected through human love. And all of these things he found highly offensive. And they gave him electric shock therapy after he tried to grab the Bible off the therapist so he could read some scripture. In fact he quickly got a reputation for being highly unstable and dangerous such was his anguish at not been given access to the things he loved.

And every night in his mind he would cry out to God in confusion and desperation. And every night the storm remained and lashed against the glass of his window and rattled the wooden shutters.

The second week was filled with lessons on how Hell was empty and that doubt was crucial for a person's wellbeing. All of which he found utter nonsense and unhelpful especially the teachings on how Constantine had masculinised the church and how God had allowed two forbidden lovers entry into heaven on a one night pass in a drug-induced dream.

And every night of that week he would grow angry with God for bringing him to such a god-forsaken place. And every night the lightning flashed down from the clouds and scorched the land.

On the third week he heard stories about God's love for interfaith couples and transgender people and how Jesus never actually healed anyone, and he felt violated in his spirit. When they told him that Jesus was conceived in the same way that every other baby had been, he became genuinely concerned for their well-being and the salvation of their souls. And all the while, the lights of the centre flickered on and off as the power struggled in the storm.

On the fourth week they broke the doctrinal holds over him, cast out his prejudices, showed him the horror of the cross erected outside Auschwitz and tied him to a chair and blasted a water cannon at him until finally, after 28 days, he and the storm broke.

"How do you feel?" asked God when they discharged him the next day into bright sunlight.

"Tired and exhausted," said the man. "So much so that it seems that I am now imagining talking to you."

"This is a good place for your soul," said God looking at the mountains surrounding the lake. "The Romans were the first to plant vineyards here. Do you like a glass or two of wine?"

The man nodded, "I used to."

"You didn't want your old stuff back when you checked out?" said God.

"No, I don't need them anymore."

"Try reading this," said God passing him a copy of Mary Shelley's *Frankenstein*.

"A novel?"

"Yes. You really have no idea where you are have you?"

"No, not really."

"What was the worst part?" said God.

"Sundays were hard. I didn't know what to do with myself."

"I play video games on Sundays," said God. "You should come hang out with me."

"Why did you do it?" said the man. "Send me here, that is."

"You asked me to. And you did really well. Many go through the rehab and never want anything to do with me ever again. Burning away Prometheus' blinkers from their eyes leaves many bitter and awakes the monster within them."

"I had no idea what I had become," said the man. "I really didn't. I'm sorry."

"It's okay," said God gazing out over the waters. "No one is born that way. That is what your addiction and a lack of love produce. You will find your critical thinking and capacity for independent thought have been seriously stunted. I will help you with that."

Out above the lake a golden eagle swooped from the sky and intercepted a spy drone that was following dragon boats as they skimmed over the waters.

God smiled and said, "Do you think it was worth it?"

"Yes."

"Are you thirsty?"

"No, not with you here."

"No," said God gesturing towards a large table under the shade of an ancient olive tree, "I meant do you want a drink?"

"Is this him?" said one of the two women who were already sitting there, drinking wine.

"It is indeed," said God.

"We are so excited to meet you," said the first woman holding out her hand; her face full of freckles and smiles.

"Er, thanks," said the man.

"This is Melodie and Jane," said God introducing them. "They are planning their honeymoon."

"We have decided that it should be a voyage on the Argo to search for giants!" said Melodie.

"You must come to the wedding," said Jane and handed him a glass of wine.

Smiling the man drank and there, surrounded by the beauty of the lake and the grandeur of the Alpine peaks, he felt like he had been reborn.

And there was evening, and there was a new morning.

And it was good.

Very good indeed.

Speaking from Northern Ireland, the President said after learning of the crash, "We hope for the best, and we are deeply grieved that this has occurred."

An airline spokeswoman said the Geneva-bound jetliner plummeted into the ocean killing all aboard and the victims' names would be posted on the airline's website.

And so the stories stopped.
And the wine was all gone.

The memory of tears holds you motionless for a moment **you are infected** you consider if you can ever find the will to move again **the disease spreading throughout your body** as you imagine your heart fragmenting you **resist the urge to simplify the profound** a million pieces within you and **only your heart can save you** as you pull yourself up out of the silt you stand for a moment in the sunlight **there is joy and there is pain** shaking your head you force yourself to think divergently to move **lightness and darkness** away from what is expected and find a way again **this is a dream** reinventing itself and **it is not a dream** embrace internal conflicts by following your heart and remember **it is death** as you stride out across the dark mafic landscape to find your way home **and it is life…**

When the man saw that the fruit of the tree was good

for food and pleasing to the eye, and also desirable

for gaining wisdom, he took some and ate it.

He also gave some to his wife, who was with him,

and she ate it.

Here's Your Story
In Seventy Seconds

A sediment covering the truth. Layers of decay that have sunk slowly down through time. You lose sight of who you are in shit and broken dreams. Fear keeps the machine grinding sinew and bone and prevents you rising up to return home. Which way from here? Let's make a list of assent to a dumbed-down reality and kneel down in silent and indifferent hate. Send the child in your heart down into the pit to bring you back worm-infested water they call life. Feel the sickness and vomit yourself senseless in the desert filled with fresh water. A repository of dogma in a septic tank just for you as you wonder what was it you were supposed to do. Lock the doors and run like hell. That would be a start. Favourite contradictions and mixed feelings. The love of silent films. Russia wins. The amazing force of quantum consciousness. The Universe may be one entity and aware of itself. Are you alone? Excellent use of aggressive robotic updates. Here's your story in seventy seconds. Art from antiquity tearing you apart. You know it needs to be done. This has been a major scandal. Here's what you could accomplish if you had the US military's $600 billion budget. Magnetic activity spotted on the Sun. A beautiful place to trip. More evidence of life and now it has gone.

The Secret of Eternal Flight

My lover is hidden within the darkness of an eternal night,
with no dawn.
Only a golden thread holds us together,
and I fear that it will break.

When I ask, why is it that I am made this way?
I take a moment to feel the beat of my heart,
and know that I have no control over such things.
I look instead to the flow of the river to the sea,
and abandon myself to the enormity,
of the unknown.

The beauty we seek is sown on the ground,
on the mountain on which we were born.
We were built for high flying you and I,
with our internal morphological tweaks.
A rapid ascent and I remember how I felt,
when you told me we would never die.

This then is to love:
It is to be taken down into the warmth of the mud,
and to hold my breath,
hoping to find you.
In the dark we were woven and in the light we will be reborn.
All things come full circle,
and at the end of our journey,
we will know the secret of eternal flight.

You have no say in when your journey begins. Indeed you can't even remember when and where your journey began. Not first-hand anyway. Only by the stories you have been told. And you have no recollection of anything at all before you came into being. And that doesn't worry you.

It did worry Aeternitas.

She spent hours every day thinking about the billions of years when she hadn't existed. And of all the things she had missed, of all the wonders she had not witnessed and of the people she had never got a chance to know or to fall in love with. And her memories before her birth were formless and desolate and she felt lost in total darkness.

And so she allowed herself to imagine a time before her.

And those imaginings became stories.

And those stories became truths in her heart.

It came to pass that God saw those stories within Aeternitas. And her stories were full of love and light. Give Aeternitas a foothold, God thought, however small, and she would stream a whole cosmos of hope from despair, like a collapsed star pulsing out light into the darkness. And this greatly pleased God, because God had made Aeternitas and put these things inside her.

And so God took Aeternitas' imaginations about the creation of the Universe and breathed life into them. And the world was truly amazing and teamed with all kinds of life full of drama, beauty, sadness and tragedy. They were profound and they were awe inspiring.

Now it came to pass that God so loved these stories that he fashioned humans to live in them.

And it was so.

The humans though were not like the animals and they desired to know where they had come from. Why did their journey begin here? What about all the time before that when they hadn't existed?

And so the humans allowed themselves to imagine the past.

And those imaginings became stories.

And those stories became truths in their hearts.

Now God saw those stories and fell in love with them. And so God made rooms in his house where those realities existed. And they were amazing because God had made the humans and put these things inside them.

And so this cycle of creation continued until there was an infinite amount of stories without end.

But these things do not concern you because you had no say in where and when your journey began. And you have no recollection of anything at all before you came into being. And that doesn't worry you. But you can hear the stories that are told to you. And these stories brought you to this moment.

Where you are now asking this…

Do I believe?

And if you are truly exceptional.

And you are.

You are imagining your own stories.

And those stories are becoming truths in your heart.

And God is breathing life into them.

One thing is certain…

Parables

you

are not

alone

Acknowledgements

Thanks to these wonderful people for their help and encouragement...

Anna Lincoln Mockingbird, Albert Mockingbird, Terrain, Andrei Korolyov, Mark and my husband, Umberto who has been my constant source of strength and my encourager.

I also found these books really helpful and helped me in what was an unexpected journey...

The Orthodox Heretic by Peter Rollins
Sum: Forty tales from the afterlives by David Eagleman

ELSEWHEN PRESS

delivering outstanding new talents in speculative fiction

Visit the Elsewhen Press website at elsewhen.press for the latest information on all of our titles, authors and events; to read our blog; find out where to buy our books and ebooks; or to place an order.

Sign up for the Elsewhen Press InFlight Newsletter at elsewhen.press/newsletter

Sapphira Olson

Sapphira Zhanna Olson is the author of the bestselling novel
Humans (An Assortment of Minor Defects). Born in Bryansk,
Russia, Sapphira is half Russian and half American, her father
being born in Minnesota. Tragedy struck early in her life with the
death of her twin sister when she was only six weeks old and then
again with the tragic loss of her father in the Altostratus disaster.

After the global success of *Humans*, Sapphira withdrew from
public life for a number of years and this is her first work since
then. When not writing she spends her time scuba diving and
exploring, with her husband, the cold wastelands of Antarctica.